Swords and Kisses

Laurie Brady

Swords and Kisses

Swords and Kisses
ISBN 978 1 76109 009 7
Copyright © Laurie Brady 2020
Cover photo by Ian on Unsplash

First published 2020 by
Ginninderra Press
PO Box 3461 Port Adelaide 5015
www.ginninderrapress.com.au

Yet each man kills the thing he loves,
By each let this be heard,
Some do it with a bitter look,
Some with a flattering word.
The coward does it with a kiss,
The brave man with a sword!

'The Ballad of Reading Gaol' – Oscar Wilde

1

Watching someone asleep is disarming. It might be that the vulnerability of the sleeper is often recast as innocence, making them look as if they need protection. Probably so, at least for the romantic. When a man loves a woman, the picture of her at peace takes on an aura of purity and beauty that has so many layers of feeling, it's hard to describe.

These were his thoughts as he left the bed, careful not to disturb the bedding and awaken her. He moved quietly to the balcony door, slid it open silently, and turned once again to watch her sleeping. She was lying on her back, well on her own side of the bed, her hair an unruly blonde bush spread on the pillow, her eyelids giving the occasional gentle flutter as if stirred by a faint electrical impulse, or perhaps a dream. Her cheeks were rouged by the warmth of sleep, and the morning sun from the open curtains that spilled like honey on the carpet.

He watched from the balcony door, an image so charged with feeling, he was overcome, mesmerised by the sheet that covered her evident female shape, and that was pulled to her chin, rising and falling rhythmically with her breathing.

The hotel balcony at Terrigal had a view of the ocean and the swell of water caressing the sand, repetitive and relentless, marking time as surely as the tick of a clock. A row of statuesque fir trees stood like sentinels along the beach front. He'd been here before and seen the sepia prints browned by the years, circa 1922, the battered cardboard-backed photos you find on some rummage table of bric-a-brac at a ladies' fundraiser, or even glossily resurrected for the town's centenary in olive coloured mounts. The trees were there then, just the same, immutable like the waves.

He stood in a lemony rhomboid printed by wintry sun, wearing the hotel's terry-towelling robe, and leaning against the balcony rail. The ocean was a mass of crystals in the early morning sun beyond the plush of deep green leaves. He watched the cars crawling up the hill out of town to Avoca, and a woman walking two golden-haired retrievers. The town was coming to life.

A sound or just an awareness alerted him and he turned to the door to see her sitting on the side of the bed and yawning. A full-length nightie failed to disguise the shapeliness of her body.

'Good morning,' he said brightly.

'Morning,' she answered softly without looking in his direction.

'Sleep well?'

'Mmmm.' Code for 'yes'.

How he wanted to go to her, move to the side of the bed and wait till she stood in front of him, or lift her to standing, and hold her, feel the heat of her, and breathe her smell of warm wool and pine. But he felt it wouldn't be welcome. How he wished she'd come to him with a hug, a touch or even a meaningful look. She wouldn't.

It had taken several months to convince her to come away with him, to convince her that intimacy didn't have to mean sex. She'd evaded giving an answer to his appeals, and he knew better than to ask for reasons. They weren't naïve. Having a night together in a resort hotel and sharing a bed carried implicit messages, and she baulked at the presumption. But she came.

He wanted more. He wondered if she would find the freedom of being away intoxicating, that it might open and free something inside her that was closed. He would never force things. She knew that.

She'd climbed into bed last evening before he'd undressed, and rolled onto her side. He'd approached like the nervous and unvintaged husband on his wedding night. He lay on one side of the bed, while she was far away on the other. It could only have been a message. When he began to talk, she rolled onto her back out of politeness to listen, and his fingers walked his hand slowly across the divide till he found her hand. She didn't resist it being held.

She was silent at first. He made idle talk about what they'd done during the day, and how he'd enjoyed the evening meal at Sea Salt. He probed for her approval. Her answers were courteous but stopped short of excitement. She had enjoyed herself. The dinner was great.

He wondered if he could move closer to her, feel the heat of her arm or thigh, even lock legs. But there was nothing about her talk that was inviting, and nothing that was forbidding. They stopped talking. She had nothing else to say. She was tired.

'Good night,' she said after a long silence, 'and thank you.' She rolled back onto her side, facing away from him, curled into a foetal position.

The curtains were drawn. It was black in the room and quiet except for the faint hum of the air conditioner. How he would have loved to curl up behind her, mould his body to hers, feel her warmth, smell the scent of her hair. But darkness doesn't disguise or excuse intention.

He first met her in the supermarket. 'Sorry about the cliché,' he laughed, when he later told the story of their meeting and saw Troy smile. 'But wait till you hear the rest.'

They were shopping in the same aisle, and she'd dropped a box of dog food. He crouched to pick it up. She knelt at the same time. Their heads didn't collide, but he felt the sway of blonde hair smack the side of his face like a soft glove. Smelled the lavender. They rose together, both with a hand on the box of dog food, and nearly collided again.

'I think this is yours,' he said, embarrassed, feeling like an intruder, butting in where he wasn't wanted. Why say anything? Explanations weren't called for.

'Thanks,' she offered without looking at him, and taking the box.

'What sort of dog do you have?' he asked, regretting it immediately because she'd already turned to go. She was on her way. He thought his question might have rescued an awkward situation, or opened a welcome one.

'Sorry,' she said, already facing away yet stopping for a moment. 'Someone's waiting,' and she headed for the checkout with a determined look, clutching her purchases to her body and walking quickly.

He watched her retreat from the aisle as the natural world of wheeled trolleys, cashier's announcements, chiding mothers and traffic noise returned.

The thought of her persisted throughout the day. Rather than fade, the picture of her became more defined as memory created and recreated images. The dimple beside her mouth, the one small shell-like ear not hidden by blonde hair, the slender fingers that held the dog food box printed themselves on his mind. In idle moments, he invented less clumsy and pleasurable scenarios of meeting her in the supermarket.

Over the next week, his thoughts of her didn't recede. Sometimes his memory would sprint ahead and invent romantic scenarios, and then swerve dangerously to consider more likely realities. She'd shown no interest in him at all, her 'thanks' was almost dismissive, and she'd hurried away as if threatened. But he became a more frequent visitor to the supermarket, only buying one or two items each time he went in the hope of seeing her.

He did see her there a week later. She was wearing black slacks, a soft cotton blouse of sky blue and black track shoes. He watched her from a distance, changing aisles to keep her in sight, darting to and fro, and wondering what security people watching the shoppers from concealed cameras would make of his antics.

She bought vegetables, pasta, fruit, oats and elseve balsam, and his imagination worked overtime constructing her life, defining her from her purchases.

He followed her from the supermarket, keeping a safe distance. She was walking quickly, looking fixedly ahead, her bag over a shoulder, changing her shopping from hand to hand. Cars sped by, a helicopter hovered a block away. An infant sat on the pavement screaming, refusing his mother's entreaties. The sky was off-white and glaring.

Why am I doing this, he asked himself. It was more than casual interest. Was it infatuation? Why was he so drawn to her? He'd had girlfriends before, girls who had piqued his interest, girls who had excited his desire. He wasn't naïve, but he'd never felt like this. His few relationships had blossomed and died with little pain beyond a hint of regret or an easily restored ego.

'What's this need in me?' he'd later ask Troy, stressing the 'me'. 'Cavorting around the suburbs, following a woman…you could say stalking a woman. Is it love? I know love is a chameleon word, always changing colour to fit different circumstances. Besides, I don't know her.' Yet even in his early twenties, love for him was an absolute, beyond time or taint.

She crossed at the lights, and he was too far behind to catch the 'walk', and had to watch her turning right on the other side of the street.

Just as well, he said to himself, believing he'd lost her, his recent thoughts supporting the belief that his feelings were a loveless obsession that would disappear with time. But as he waited at the lights, he saw her enter a bookstore sixty metres further down the street.

He approached uncertainly and stood near the door where she couldn't see him, watching her behind the counter, already serving a customer. This was where she worked. Another customer was waiting, and he thought better of approaching.

'Hello, Tiffany,' the older woman who must have been a regular greeted her, and then he was too far away to hear the chat about the woman's book selection.

Tiffany. Her name was Tiffany. Her naming gave her weight, an identity that was no longer fanciful but real. He'd say it over the following weeks, sometimes repeatedly, savouring its taste.

For the next few days, he debated whether to see her again, always knowing that he would. The images didn't fade, and he began to see his feeling, or was it his obsession, as love. Why her? There didn't seem to be anything exceptional about her. Do we ever have a choice of who to love?

He sat at his study desk, and tried to make a list, to tease out the pros and cons of a relationship, to give some substance or authority to his feeling. He couldn't. It didn't work. He didn't know enough about her. And for what he did know, she didn't seem to tick many boxes.

There was no one waiting outside at nine a.m. when the doors of the bookshop were opened. She was already there. He was feeling a tightness in his chest. A panic gripped him. He thought of taking a box of dog food, the same one he'd seen her buy at the supermarket. It might look too forced, too contrived, so he abandoned the idea. Besides, the dog mightn't even belong to her.

She was behind the counter and didn't look up, so he wandered around the shelves, looking for a book, occasionally opening one and turning a few pages with false interest, trying to manage the tension he felt with heavy breathing.

'Can I help you?' she asked as he approached, with no look of recognition. Her blouse was crisp, her hair sheeny.

He put the latest Tim Winton on the counter.

'A good choice,' she continued. 'I enjoyed it.'

'You probably don't remember,' he began falteringly. 'We met in the supermarket a few weeks ago. We nearly collided over a box of dog food.' He forced a smile. Humour might be a way in.

She looked up, searching his face. Her confusion was apparent in glassy eyes. 'Oh, did we?' she said, and began to process the sale. She didn't appear comfortable.

'I wonder if you would like to have dinner one day after work.' There, it was said. The weeks had been leading up to it. He kept looking down at the counter, afraid of what he might see in her face, and when he finally looked up, he saw her shaking her head.

His heart stopped. 'I'm sorry,' he stammered, already moving away. 'It wasn't very thoughtful of me to…' and he didn't continue. He didn't know why it wasn't thoughtful. Her reaction said otherwise.

She leant over the counter. 'My boyfriend,' she began, and for the first time looked at him intently, her eyes boring into him.

'Of course. Of course. I understand.' It was time to retreat. A customer had entered. 'My name is Michael,' he said hurriedly. 'I come in here every Friday after school. I teach at the primary school. I can be contacted…' but why say any more? Why make such an appeal? It was over. Even telling her he came in every Friday wasn't true.

He came to the bookshop for the next two Fridays and felt he was intruding. She nodded once in his direction but that was all. Was it possible that she hadn't seen him? He realised she was probably regarding him as coercive, so he stopped coming.

He played tennis on Wednesday nights, exercised in the mornings in his garage, read the Tim Winton before turning out the bedside light, cooked pasta, and prepared his fourth-grade lessons for school. The days passed, hot, windy, overcast, wet, eventful, demanding, boring, all slipping into the amnesia of history.

But he did remember her, the little dimple beside her mouth, the cool and slender fingers on the box of dog food, and her blonde hair brushing his cheek. And he remembered the intent, even curious look she gave him when he asked her out, a look of appraisal.

A month later, the school secretary called him to the phone.

It was Tiffany. 'Thursday's good for me,' she said, speaking softly. She seemed as uncomfortable as he had been all those weeks earlier. 'If you still want to, you can pick me up from work at six p.m.,' and the phone went dead. She hadn't waited for an answer.

Her call raised many questions, but he was waiting for her outside the bookshop on Thursday, indecently early. He'd spent ages getting ready. They went to a restaurant she knew two blocks away.

'Is everything all right with you?' He asked as they ate, trying to sound casual.

'Why wouldn't it be?' she queried, and he realised he'd confronted her.

'The boyfriend. Does he mind? I don't want to…' He was aware of the need to tread carefully.

'It doesn't matter to Paul,' she answered.

He'd later see the meal as a success. She told him a little of herself. Born in a rural town in New South Wales he'd never heard of, to ageing parents who'd married late, she was the youngest of three girls. She did particularly well at the local high school, completed a secretarial course, and was immediately employed in a branch of the Public Service. But while her superiors and the staff were kind, she found the work stifled her spirit.

That, and what she believed to be a small-town mentality, prompted her move to Sydney, where she hoped to get enough money to study Arts at a university. That hadn't happened yet because circumstances she didn't reveal hadn't been kind, but it was still her goal. She hoped to be accepted as a mature-age student.

He did most of the talking, but was acutely aware of not blowing his own trumpet. She did show an interest in the up and down side of teaching.

Immediately after their dessert, she stood, waiting for him to help her into her coat. 'I must be going,' she said. 'Next Thursday? I can meet you here.'

He offered to walk her home, or get a taxi, but she declined.

'But I'd like…'

'No, Michael, not necessary,' and then to soften the ultimatum, 'really.'

So they began to meet on Thursdays. He waited patiently outside the restaurant, and she was always on time. He bought chocolate one time, flowers another. She was polite thanking him, but he felt she was embarrassed, so he stopped. She always left abruptly, insisting on walking home by herself. He accepted her decision, realising that Paul was probably waiting, possibly having given her a curfew. He felt jealous but there was satisfaction in thinking that she might be taking a risk for him.

He had no doubt now that it was love. Little things he'd never noticed took on fresh meaning: the last of the winter dew caught in silver by the sun, the budding of the roses outside his window, the heady smell of jasmine. He was alive on Thursdays as their night approached, quiet and reflective on Fridays, philosophical over the weekend, and brightening as the new week began.

After several Thursday dinners, she took his hand as they left the restaurant, and began to walk with him in the direction she usually walked alone. She didn't explain, and he thought it best not to ask, and not to show either surprise or pleasure.

Her unit was on the ground floor of a three-storey block in a quiet street, with a small garden at the front. She opened the door and entered. He followed. She headed for the kitchen without a word to boil the kettle. He didn't follow but sat on one corner of the beige lounge. The room was sparsely yet tastefully furnished with a teak coffee table, a small circular occasional table with a lithe-looking and naked brass woman-cum-lamp base with an apricot shade, and two modern wall prints. A single framed colour photograph of a man and woman was all that adorned the sideboard. The woman was Tiffany. The man was tall and dark, possibly Spanish or Italian.

'Yes, it's Paul,' she said, anticipating his question, seeing him looking at the photograph as she entered the room with two cups of coffee.

'He's not here tonight?' He framed the obvious as a question that gave her licence to answer how she wanted.

'He liked Tim Winton too,' she replied, not answering the question. She seemed to be distracted.

'Will he be back tonight?' he asked, and realised that she would see his question as a test or an affront, a way of determining if 'the coast was clear'. 'Will I have the pleasure of meeting him?' He hurried to redeem himself.

'Paul's gone,' she answered, sipping her coffee with a trembling hand.

He said nothing. He'd learnt his lesson. He could console her, offer hope, or suggest that everything might be for the better, that there was a reason for everything. Both were slippery slopes. So they sipped their coffee in silence for a few minutes.

'I miss him so much,' she finally said. 'He died, two years ago.'

'I'm so sorry,' he said, taken by surprise, and waited for her to say more. But she had nothing else to add, and stood, looking down at him. 'Thank you for a nice night.' There was no doubt about her intentions. 'Next Thursday?' She proceeded him to the door, gave him a quick dry kiss on the cheek, and quickly closed the door after him.

He walked home beneath a near-full moon, and in a balmy breeze thick with the flowery scents of spring, feeling alternately pleased and depressed. Paul was no real competition. The jealousy he'd felt when she first spoke his name was groundless. He was no longer part of the equation. Or was he? Even absent, Paul still seemed to be a part of her life. But how great was his influence? Was it just a case of love's backward-looking tendency to make a myth of itself?

'I think I understand,' Troy said, having listened intently to Michael's early story about his relationship with Tiffany. 'I haven't ever been that infatuated. I love Stephanie, I love her very much, but it isn't as all-consuming as what you've told me. Perhaps if she didn't show any interest…'

'It is rather all-consuming, isn't it?' Michael smiled. It was important to step outside his obsession, to hear the sane voice of another male. It was a reality check.

'I think I more than most people can understand how someone can have a lasting influence over another person,' Troy was sombre, 'how someone like this fellow Paul can exert control even beyond the grave.'

They were silent for a minute. There was a lot to digest. And Michael didn't want to stir up painful memories.

'Do you think that there are things we cannot change?' Michael's comment was a question and a statement. 'Is it that everything is already written, and we're programmed to follow?'

'No,' Troy answered vehemently. 'I hate to think that we don't have freedom to make decisions, to change the course of things. It's frightening to think that we're all puppets on strings being worked by…worked by…'

'I'm with you,' Michael added, wondering at the passion of Troy's protest. 'I like to think we have the capacity to help ourselves, whether we choose to do so, or not…'

There was a further long pause. The two friends were not uncomfortable with silence.

'There has to be a purpose,' Troy continued. His concern had become more far-reaching. 'Some big design…' His voice trailed away.

Michael and Troy had started school together, and as near-neighbours, caught the same green and cream bus that wheezed its way up hills and around tight bends to shudder to a stop at the local primary school. They played the obligatory games of marbles, sharing their spoils, collected cigarette cards and matchbox toys, swapped conversation lollies with their favoured girls, and were both flautists in the school band, driven to community celebrations by one of the mothers, dressed in their navy wool shorts, white shirts, tartan sashes and navy school-crested caps, to be lauded by dignitaries who smiled benignly and espoused specious optimism about the future of the next generation.

The sexes were separated on different campuses at their primary school. They couldn't even mingle. In their final year, their class would meet each week with a class of fifth year girls for folk dancing. They'd laugh years later, saying it must have been a syllabus decree to interact before waking hormones consigned them all to heterosexual hell. The first class to arrive would stand on the inner of two concentric circles painted on the asphalt. If the boys were there first, the girls were required to stand behind a partner, without seeming to seek a particular boy. So the freely amplified static was the first music for their budding romanticism. They were both bewitched. The girls were soft and compelling. They smelt different.

They had started cubs together, supplementing the virtues of reverence and cleanliness with those of community service and honest toil through the annual bob a job responsibilities, and they played in both their cubby houses at weekends when Michael wasn't required to help his father in the garden, and Troy wasn't forced to practise the piano.

The rules in those days were incontestable, particularly those at school, and beyond the understanding of young children, so they rarely questioned them, never made a fuss, though unlike Michael's own inflexible faith in adult infallibility, Troy often suffered punishment for his irrelevant inquiries, or his often-sullen behaviour that emerged in the later primary school years.

Perhaps it is the way of all children to fashion friendship for their own different ends, like the cubbyhouse games that shift direction as each player takes a turn in assuming control over the action. And yet Michael and Troy's ends were not dissimilar. They didn't fight, probably because disagreements were rare and never intense enough to be divisive.

Troy was a slight boy with a spray of freckles, and a mop of sandy hair that hung over one side of his face and needed a vigorous shake of the head to remove from hiding his eyes. His shyness was apparent from a lack of conviction and the way he avoided meeting another's eyes in conversation. He grew to be robust, even powerful-looking, with puberty, though the shyness was converted to a lack of certainty that was sometimes seen and valued by girls as vulnerability or humility.

One event in their mid-primary school years helped to define the nature of their relationship, though the foundations were already laid. A substantial amount of money went missing from the day's takings at the school canteen, and Russell Nicholson was identified as the culprit. He was hauled protesting his innocence to the principal's office. Troy and Michael saw Russell's distraught mother entering the school to plead for her son. But it was to no avail, and Russell was expelled.

They later learned that Tim Addison was the single witness who had identified Russell, and were able to browbeat a confession from him that he was the thief. He had avoided blame by naming another, never considering that the consequences would be so severe. But he would never admit what he told them to anyone else. His punishment would be double that of Russell. He felt guilty, he was really sorry, but not brave enough to change places.

Russell was their close friend, and their pleadings and threats to Tim to accept the blame fell on deaf ears. There was no point telling the principal who the real culprit was. Tim would deny it.

Stung by this incident, Michael and Troy made a pact. They agreed to be completely honest with each other, even if being honest caused the other pain.

'My father used to say that a hurtful truth is better than a harmful lie,' Michael said.

'And,' Troy added, 'let's agree to share our real thoughts and feelings without waiting to be asked. We won't hide anything.'

They shook hands feeling very grown-up.

2

Born in Sydney to caring parents, Michael Manton lived in a new satellite suburb of Sydney where all families enjoyed a similar lifestyle, and so avoided invidious social comparisons. His father worked as an accountant, and his mother didn't work, freeing her to drive the two children to their after-school activities, to assist on the school canteen, and to practise a mild protectiveness over Michael and his younger sister Amity.

Michael was fair-haired with angelic blue eyes that seemed to reveal constant curiosity, but in later years became windows to his innermost feelings, as long as the watcher was sensitive enough to read them. He always wanted to please, and would later question whether this was nobility or simply his own need, and whether it made a difference.

His infant years were an endless blur, because the only benchmarks were night and day, and for the young Michael they weren't part of any bigger scheme of calibrating life. Dinner, when he asked his mother, thinking it was getting dark, might be 'soon', whatever that meant, or 'Not for a while yet, Michael. You've only just had lunch.'

His parents sometimes went out at night, his father in a black suit and a white shirt with a stiff collar that did up at the front with little buttons, and his mother in a shiny silver dress that caught the light and wouldn't let go, with her hair all done up on top of her head, and smelling like the jasmine that hung over the cubby house where he played with Amity. He'd hug his mother before she left, careful not to crush her dress, calmed by the coolness of her touch, heady with her perfume.

He'd be taken with Amity to Grandma Gladys and Aunt Doris, who lived in a big federation house around the corner. He'd be given a pink musk stick and a fizzy orange drink, played snap and sevens with Grandma and Auntie, was put in a big double bed with Amity, and was later carried to the car by his father in the early morning when it was black and cold outside.

'I was awake,' he'd tell his mother in the morning, as if it were proof of being grown-up. 'Amity wasn't,' he'd say with pride.

His memory would cling to the special occasions like birthdays and Christmas with candles on a cake, plum puddings with brandy sauce or ice cream, party games with his cousins, and the presents he'd arrange on his bed to show Amity and his parents.

There were other memorable events too, like the day his father brought home Whisky, a Labrador puppy; the awful day Grandma Gladys 'passed away' and he wanted to know where she'd gone; and the time he and Amity both fell when a tree branch they had climbed on in the backyard broke. Both his knees were badly grazed and bleeding. Amity suffered a heavy bump to her thigh that would probably become a bruise. Their mother came to the rescue, concerned that Amity might have done some serious damage. She fetched bandages, cotton wool swabs and Dettol to bathe Michael's wounds.

Amity sobbed. 'It hurts, Mummy,' she kept saying.

'I know, darling,' Mother soothed, 'but it'll stop hurting soon, and we'll have one of Daddy's special chocolates.'

Michael tried as hard as he could to be brave, yet his knees hurt. The blood was trickling into his socks. And, as suffering is often infectious between children, he began to whimper.

'It's all right, Mikey.' His mother patted his head affectionately and ruffled his hair. 'Little soldiers never cry.'

It was several Thursdays before she invited him back to her place, though the invitation was more a taking of his hand and heading in the right direction rather than a polite request. He'd invited her to his place a few times, but she'd avoided answering rather than refused outright. He hadn't pressed the matter.

They walked in silence. The streets were empty and there was an eerie calm like that preceding a storm. Lights dazzled from an approaching car, and illuminated a purple sky. Their previous Thursdays had been pleasant, and they had fallen into a routine of starting with drinks, asking each other about the preceding week, ordering the meal, discussing work and revealing plans for the future.

But not shared plans. He had tried to hint at a future together a couple of times, but when she read his face and sensed the drift of his words, they were severed by a glance.

He told her about Amity and the importance of his parents in his life. She told him about her sisters, and their contentment with the narrow life of a small rural town that she had found stifling.

His thoughts conflicted as they walked. Was the approaching storm portentous? Did she feel that their relationship had reached a new threshold, one that welcomed greater intimacy? There was nothing in her manner to suggest so.

She was in the kitchen making coffee when the storm arrived. Thunder bellowed, lightning knifed the dark, rain lashed the windows and the wind shrilled like a small boy's tin whistle. She seemed disconcerted, perhaps because it would not be considerate to send him home in such weather. He could see her dilemma but said nothing.

'It was a road accident,' she said, handing him a cup before sitting down, and taking her first sip of coffee.

'Sorry?' His mind was slow to understand.

'Paul. I always told him he drove too fast, but he wouldn't listen. Never took any bloody notice.' Her face contorted and she began to sob, loud rasping sounds that shook her body, and made him feel helpless. Her mug of coffee clattered on the table and spilled. 'I hate him. Why wouldn't he listen? Why wouldn't he? Why?'

She turned to Michael with a face he could barely recognise, as if he could provide the answer, as if things were that simple. He felt ashamed to feel desire when it was compassion that she needed. He wanted to hold her. That was a statement in itself. It would be a badge of intimacy, and if she returned his need, a sign of relenting. He wanted to tell her that he would help her through it all, that they would do this together, but it was clear that she didn't want to be held, and she didn't want to be told.

'A tree. Hit a tree,' she blubbered. 'His fault. Silly bugger. Terrible speed, the police said. Car smashed beyond recognition.' Her words were coming in haemorrhaged fragments. 'Lived for a few hours…called me…hospital…held him as he died.'

Her outburst was over as suddenly as it had started. She stopped sobbing, blew her nose and dabbed at her eyes with a napkin. Rain thrashed the windowpanes, and a wind whistled, blowing a branch against the glass pane with repeated drumming.

'Is there anything…' he began, watching her closely, and saw her shaking her head. She was back to her normal self, as if nothing unusual had happened.

They sat for several minutes in silence. He was awash with different emotions, concern, desire, even jealousy. Paul might be gone, but was there any greater bond you could share with someone than the awful intimacy of death?

'You'd better stay here,' she said, getting to her feet. 'The lounge won't be comfortable, so I suppose…' The words trailed after her to the bedroom, hovering like vapour in the air.

He waited till she returned, wanting to stay, but wondering if he should offer to depart and leave her alone, to at least offer to see if the storm abated.

She returned dressed in a nightie with small rose-coloured flowers stitched around the neck. Bare feet. She looked composed. 'I'm going to bed,' she said. 'I hope you don't mind. Can you turn the light off when you come.'

He didn't hurry. There was no need. It was hardly a whole-hearted invitation. When he climbed gently into the bed, she was already asleep, lying on her side with her head half-covered by the doona. He lay on his back, eyes facing the ceiling, where shadowed patterns of filigree formed and re-formed.

Even lying in a bed next to her, he felt more depressed than he had in weeks. There was no desire. She was closed to him. Surely relationships are about incremental creep, he reasoned. About concessions made and returned with interest. A man says he'd like to see more of a woman, and she says how lovely that would be; she admits to love, and he tells her she means the earth to him; he kisses her gently, and she takes him in her arms. That he thought to be true, but the man and woman had to feel the same.

Michael began to look back over the relationship. Was it that he hadn't done enough? She had to know how he felt. Had he ever told her that he loved her? He knew he'd tried, but any emotion of that kind, any look that foreshadowed such a statement, was met with chill. Perhaps the fault was all with him. Was he wrapping himself in a cloak of protectiveness? No!

It was becoming clearer to him that she didn't love him. If only she could. If only she could bring herself to admit love for him, to shape the feeling into words, the deluge would begin. Words were dams that held and released feelings.

All that lay ahead of him now was a snarl of desire and broken sleep.

The local boys' high school didn't have a girls' school nearby, and there weren't many social opportunities for a young teenager. For Michael, sexual awakening bedded down with idealism. He grew seven inches in his fourteenth year to a respectable stature, and began twice-weekly shaving. Hormonal changes generated a sexual interest spiced by church-belt forbidden-fruits theology.

When he turned fifteen, his father, probably wanting to catch him alone, not so much from the need for man-to-man, or man-to-soon-to-be-man talk, but from embarrassment, handed him a small hard cover book, *Attaining Manhood*, telling him that if he had any questions… His quick retreat belied the invitation. The book gave a technical account of reproduction, opening midriffs with internal black line drawings, but said nothing about the dynamic of sex. The talk of eggs being fertilised reminded him of the warm hard-shelled tokens of sex that he collected from the chooks that scavenged in their own filth in the hen house.

There were other books too, an eclectic collection in his father's small library. Among the Kant, Descartes, Darwin and Emerson, he read Marcus Aurelius and the Persian polymath Rhazes under headings that suggested something provocative to slake his need, passages that praised the benefits of abstinence or warned that masturbation would cause blindness.

His social activities were confined to a church-based youth group of sixty teenage boys and girls. It was his first real opportunity to meet girls apart from his cousins. The group held meetings at which they sang, listened to the Christian message and later attended the evening church service. Sometimes there were weekend social events that could never be missed. The ethos of the group was didactic but too uncertain of itself to be sanctimonious.

At one service following a meeting of the youth group, the rector delivered his four-point sermon (all sermons were defined by their reducibility to four points) on the biblical text of 'first you leave, then you cleave', an infallible argument against the evil of premarital sex. Girls, unlucky in love, were guilty of more than schoolgirl naughtiness. It was 'a sin of the flesh'.

In Michael's early adolescence, he began to exercise with chest expanders, tensile spring coils that were pulled apart. What he couldn't do inside, he did outside, connecting both strands of the expanders to a hook he screwed into the paling fence outside the back-porch door. There were times he exercised in heat and pouring rain, refusing to stop, despite his mother's pleas, feeling inspired by his dedication. His desire to look better changed over the years to become a renaissance ideal, the complete man, strong in mind and body.

At fifteen, Michael was given his own room, a small converted two and a half metre square sunroom off the kitchen, large enough for a desk, bed and reassuring books. But it was his, his own cloistered world where insights emerged and latent feelings simmered in a stew of wild imaginings. Everything outside was heavy with meaning, the pittosporum that thrummed on the window pane near his bed with nutty fingers; the family's television seeping blue from the hall, its canned hysterics mocking bedside prayer; and the bright luminous night sky pierced by stars. His room was the cave to which he returned to live his brimming feelings.

It was a place where he could suffer the injustices of the world and wonder at his own differentness. It never occurred to him that his peers may have endured the same isolation or wrestled with the same demons. It was also a place to nurse romantic dreams, to feel the imagined warmth of girls, and to imagine his superhero feats of rescuing them from danger. Sometimes it was a girl he knew, but more often than not they were amorous inventions. Romantic and sexual feelings were an uneasy alliance, for sex loomed as a necessary evil, something a bit naughty that salvaged respectability in marriage. This conflict was confusing for Michael. Girls were hoisted on pedestals, not just because they were less coarse, but because sex was something men did to women. Women sometimes complied, but men were the real villains.

The years changed such an uncomfortable alliance into an ideal worth pursuing that he never abandoned. Love and sex had become divine companions.

Michael was helping his father in the garden when the news came of Amity's death. She'd drowned while staying with the family of a girlfriend. She'd been pulled from the surf, and lifesavers had done CPR, but to no avail.

His first response was disbelief. Emotion sometimes saunters behind a sudden shock. The meanings need to settle. Its impact would follow, not so much as the usual show of grief, but more as an ether, a suffering without feeling that dulled his world without his being fully aware of it. It was more a challenge to his life of certainties, and the problem of making sense of it in a bigger scheme.

His parents were crushed. It was a typical coping with grief for his parents' generation, his mother's hysteria and pain without check, and his father's grim-faced stoicism and struggling faith in reason.

He'd always remember the hospital and its apricot brick, its shaved lawn and would-be cheerful flowers, the immutability and the timelessness. He felt like the covetous guardian of a tombstone.

Amity lay somewhere inside in final wooden sleep, and he found himself searching for symbols, for meanings in the sprinkler that continued to slap a spray of water onto the hospital lawn now that she was gone, and the arthritic trees continuing to flex and stretch in timeless unconcern.

His father saw the body and emerged from the mortuary annex pale and trembling about a clenched mouth. Michael didn't view the body. He'd later wonder why. He didn't need to be convinced of the terrible finality. He wanted to remember her as she'd always been. To who or what would he be saying goodbye?

In the months that followed, he'd escape to the porch at night and face the cold. The sentience of the bush with its heavy scent and cricket noises would bring her near, and he'd conspire with Amity, recalling their good times together.

'Michael Manton,' she said, introducing herself and looking spirited. 'We have something in common, Michael. I'm Michelle Murton. We're both double Ms.'

That was the beginning. Not a particularly artful approach but a welcome one, one that darted unexpectedly from behind the robes of church convention and polite guardedness, one that promised a taste of something exciting, even risqué. She was tall with red nails, skin-tight slacks and waist-length brown hair.

'I did warn you,' Troy said light-heartedly.

'Yes, you did. And we both know it wasn't going to make any difference.'

'The moving finger writes, eh?'

'Yeah, something like that.'

'No regrets, then? I don't suppose you can regret what you can't change?'

'No regrets,' but Michael seemed uncertain. 'She opened up another world for me. She broke the shackles.'

'And which world do you belong to now?'

There was a long silence before Michael replied.

'I suppose it was a rite of passage.'

'But are those rites of passage always for the better? There must be a hundred different ways, different thresholds to cross, before we arrive at …what? Maturity, I suppose.'

His relationship with Michelle had taken its rocky and inevitable course. He was a novice in affairs of the heart, and body, and she didn't mind reminding him of that.

Another long pause.

'For weeks after we separated, she cast me as the villain, implying that she was the heroine…can you believe that, can you really believe that…after all the pain…feeling nothing, like I was walking around sedated. After all those attempts to justify my behaviour that you had to suffer, I like to think I became a better person, more caring anyway.'

Troy was silent. He knew when to be quiet. It was his friend's story, even though he'd heard variations of it before, the incantation of separation.

'For months, I'd walk around the mall just to be among people. I'd feel a tenderness that was overwhelming for the exhausted mother with a bawling child, or the old bloke trying to dig coins out of his purse with arthritic fingers. I'd even go in the early morning when the street lights were still on looking like bright stars sending out golden thread in the gloom. And I'd be grateful for the fellowship of strangers, even if they said nothing. And they never did.'

Troy was uneasy. This feeling for others wasn't his experience at all. Perhaps his feelings were more focused. He hurried to change the subject. 'I remember you telling me about going back to her unit to get your overnight bag, and seeing her naked. I wonder why I thought that was so sad.'

'It was. She was hurrying from the shower. You'd think I'd be aroused, but it was so unerotic, even a bit gross, like stumbling into the fleshiness of a public change room. And she shouted at me to get out, and leave my key on the hall table. If you could have seen the venom in her face. For once, I was happy to go.'

Michael understood that he was changing his view of things as his mind kept returning to what had happened, finding new explanations, and dismissing others, using a different lens each time to interpret. It still remained raw. But he also knew that his romantic ideal was intact, not because Michelle had been the proof of it, but because she so obviously hadn't been. His ideal was stronger than ever.

'Is there anything sadder than newspapers blowing around your feet…' His voice was almost a whisper, his mind having darted elsewhere, to memories of his private hell. '…the crumpled news of yesterdays.'

Michael spent some time working out what to wear. The most wayward of children want the approval of parents even if they are loath to admit it. So it was important to make a good impression. He chose his best beige tailored slacks and teal shirt. Put on aftershave.

He was pleased. Meeting the parents was a gesture that carried a lot of weight. It was a statement of his importance to her, a way of testing family reaction to future… But enough speculation, he told himself. Don't go getting ahead of yourself. Tiffany had arranged the meeting. Her mother had come to Sydney to stay with her for several days.

'Can you come on Wednesday to my place for afternoon tea and meet my mother,' she'd said.

His heart leapt. He found himself analysing the language of the invitation. It was a bald question, most of her remarks were, but the 'can you come' was a request. It was an appeal of sorts.

He felt the last few weeks had seen an improvement between them. She'd been able to see him in the weekends, though why only now wasn't clear to him. He saw it as a welcome sign. They went to the beach twice, ate pizzas and ice cream, and walked barefoot along the sand. They held hands. It was still too cold to swim. They went to the cinema, saw *Downton Abbey* and ate popcorn, and laughed together at some of the exhibits at the Museum of Contemporary Art.

When he walked her home at night, he often said goodnight at the door, kissing her cheek that she turned to him with no reluctance. What's in a kiss, he asked himself, parodying Shakespeare. There were those that came from feeling, caring and delicate, a touch that leaves a tenderness. There were the more vigorous ones when people searched for meaning in each other's mouths. And the more voracious ones fuelled by can't-get-enough lust. So what was the exchange between himself and Tiffany? He did the kissing, if a millisecond's brushing of lips on a turned cheek could be called a kiss.

Sometimes he'd stay for a coffee, but excused himself when he thought the time was right. It was important for him that the invitation to stay came from what Tiffany really wanted, and not from a sense of duty. And even if that were never to happen, he wasn't going to force the matter.

Mrs Thurgood was not what he had expected. She was slim and sprightly. Her hair was still dark, though threaded with grey, and her face was not lined except for a faint cobweb of line beside her eyes. 'Ageing parents,' Tiffany had told him, and he'd imagined a nodding old lady with white hair as sparse as maidenhair.

'Pleased to meet you, Michael,' she said brightly, reaching out her hand. 'I've been hearing quite a lot about you.'

He stole a look at Tiffany, who was sitting on the lounge, and hoped to join her there. There might have been a curling about her mouth, a faint smile.

'It's a pleasure to meet you, Mrs Thurgood,' he answered, feeling her hand clasp his with a warmth he hadn't experienced with her daughter.

'Now, Michael, if we're going to get on,' she quipped, 'no more Mrs Thurgood. It's Margaret.'

'All right, Margaret,' he responded, 'you'd better call me Mr Manton.'

She laughed and her eyes shone.

He liked her more and more as the afternoon wore on, and he was freer with his conversation than he'd ever been when he'd been alone with Tiffany. He felt well pleased when it was time to take his leave. It had been better than he'd ever hoped it would be.

'Well, Mr Manton,' Margaret took his hand, 'I think you are going to be very good for my daughter. Very good indeed.'

Being an only child might have made people wary, particularly his teachers, because 'only' children were often regarded as mollycoddled and precious. But once people met Troy, they changed their minds. He was quiet, gentle, and while he might have shared the craving for attention of other children, he never pushed himself forward, boasted or threw a tantrum.

His father worked for the Public Service. Troy was never sure what he did. His mother didn't work, not so much from a lack of motivation, but from her husband's belief that it was the man's responsibility to support his wife.

'But I'd like to work, Colin,' she told him. 'I have the skills. I'd have no trouble getting a job, because before we were married I was…'

It was no use. For Colin, a working wife was a challenge to his masculinity.

'The very early years were good,' Troy once told Michael. 'Before I was old enough to go to school, my mother would take me shopping every Friday. She'd always say there'd be a treat for me if I was patient, and there was, a caramel milkshake, and a donut, warm and covered in sugar and cinnamon.'

Troy's talk of the early years brought back similar memories for Michael, but Troy wanted to speak. He often didn't.

'One day we saw a rocking horse in the toy section of a big department store. Can't remember which store it was. I fell in love with that horse. It had big black spots and was all shiny, painted in bright red and blue. There was a mane of soft hair on its neck. I went to climb onto it.

No, Troy, my mother said gently. I don't think that's allowed, and she took my hand and we stood looking at it for a while. It's a lot of money, Troy, my mother said as we walked away. I didn't know it at the time, but I think she was really sad. Anyway, that was just before Christmas, and when I woke up on Christmas morning, there it was, beside my bed.'

'That's a memory to treasure.' Michael was touched.

'My mother was very kind,' Troy continued. 'She never got really mad, and was always trying to find little things to do to please me.'

'And it all changed,' Michael asked, 'I mean the good years…after the incident?'

'Yeah, and more than ever after the second…incident.'

They were quiet for a minute, but their minds weren't.

'Those school years were not the happiest of times. You more than anyone knew that, Michael. I felt so helpless. That saying about having to play the cards you're dealt… Not fair, is it, if you're dealt a lousy hand.'

'No. You could ask for a redeal.' Michael tried to lighten the mood. 'But I can't see how you could cheat.'

'I went to a talk a few weeks ago.' Troy didn't seem to notice Michael's lame attempt at humour. 'One of those self-help gurus, flogging his new book. No situation is too difficult to overcome, he said, as long as you have the right attitude. Always remember, he said, the power is in your hands. And then he goes on to give his six steps. The first letters made an acronym. Something ridiculous. As if life fits a formula! And what impossible situation have you had to face, I felt like shouting out. It made me sick!'

When he was nineteen, Troy met Clara. It was his first taste of romance, or the feeling that might nurture it. She was a newly appointed work colleague at the Environmental Protection Authority, a feisty girl with violet eyes and a musical laugh. Her lively personality made her popular with her colleagues, and attractive to the shy and restrained Troy.

In the months it took to ask her out, he nursed fictions of them sharing both deep and knowing looks, and silences that meant more than words. There were erotic images as well.

They went to a restaurant with his friends and their partners where he watched her sitting with her legs crossed in a short leather skirt that revealed even more than the full length of her legs, tapping her cigarette ash into a glass while talking conceitedly, and flirting outrageously with every man in the room.

His fantasies were stricken. He lost the music of her voice, and watched her face reassemble from the sweetness he thought he knew, to something false. There was something driven, something go-getting and almost aggressive about her.

'Stephanie was my saviour,' he told Michael, who didn't doubt the good that could come from this new love.

Not so long ago, he'd been out with Stephanie himself. She was an old school friend of them both, blonde, blue-eyed and regal. She was the youngest of six children, but even as the 'baby', she hadn't been coddled. She needed quick wits and her juvenile skills of negotiation to steer a smooth course through the intrigues of her older siblings. While she had a more understated glamour and *savoir faire* than that of Clara, she didn't share her conceit and ego.

Her relationship with Michael had not been intimate. They went out several times, and stopped when Michael's studies at university became pressing, and when she had taken a long interstate holiday with her family. They had remained good friends.

'That's great, Troy,' he replied. 'I think she's perfect for you.'

Troy beamed with pleasure. It wasn't often Michael had seen his friend so pleased.

'You'd know, mate,' he replied, and they both laughed, putting their arms around each other's shoulders as they set off walking down the street. It was a rare moment of confederacy.

3

When Michael first met Troy's mother, there was a flicker of alarm before she seemed pleased that he was there. At the age of nine, he didn't know why, but later realised that she was probably concerned that he might be dragged into revealing family secrets. She must have also known that Troy needed trusted friends and the opportunity to talk to boys of his own age.

He was treated with home-made biscuits ('Do have another one, Michael') and a cup of tea. There were no cartons of flavoured milk or fizzy drinks in the Douglas home, and he found this old-fashioned and basic domesticity comforting.

Mrs Douglas watched them both closely, looking intently at each of them in turn as if she were weighing-up the nature of their relationship. Her affection for Troy was transparent, and so was his concern for her. There was pride in his voice as he introduced her, and Michael was humbled when Troy asked her what sort of day she'd had. It was a question he hadn't asked his own mother enough.

Beth Douglas was a little under average in height with a good figure, mousy-coloured hair, and a pale, aquiline face that was pretty rather than beautiful, and that didn't stand up to scrutiny, not because of her looks, but because of a self-consciousness that made her lower her milky blue eyes or turn her head when someone tried to hold her gaze. Michael liked her, not just from the nine-year-old's gratitude for biscuits, but from a warmth and gentleness that seemed to fill the room in her presence.

'I hope you'll come often, Michael,' she said, and placed a hand on his shoulder. There was a message in that touch, and in her eyes that were suddenly rheumy and wistful, though he didn't realise it then. 'Perhaps you'll join us for dinner one night,' she added, and turned away quickly.

The two boys climbed the curved staircase to Troy's bedroom, and he closed the door. Apart from Mrs Douglas, there was no one else in the house, and Michael, even at such a tender age, knew they'd be doing more than playing with his toys and games. The air was heavy with suspense. Troy needed to talk. It was only a month after their pledge to reveal their feelings.

His bed, covered with a heavy green quilt, was neatly made, but the room was a clutter of games, clothes and sporting equipment. There was a framed photograph on his bedside table showing him standing between his parents. Mrs Douglas was half inclined towards Troy and smiling. His father, dark-haired and burly, towered over them.

They sat on the bed and there was a moment's awkward silence.

'I like your mum,' Michael said, sensing the tension, and anxious to relieve it.

'Yeah, she's great,' Troy answered and, as his eyes filled with tears, he turned away.

Michael sat next to him on the bed feeling miserable and helpless. Troy's pain had become Michael's too, even though he had no idea of the cause. Grief like joy can be infectious.

That's when he told Michael the story, or rather its beginning.

Troy's father had come home at eight-thirty the night before, offering no apology for being late, reeking of alcohol and obviously belligerent. It wasn't the first time, Troy reported, so both he and his mother had cause for alarm.

'Where's my bloody dinner?' he called from the hallway before he'd entered the family room, without a word of welcome or inquiry. 'It's not bloody much for a man to expect.'

Michael imagined the burly man in the photograph on Troy's bedside table. There was no cheesy grin now. It wasn't hard to see him as formidable.

'It's in the oven, Brett,' his wife tried to appease.

And Michael could hear the kind voice that asked him to dinner, imagined her gentleness as a foil for anger, but as it so often does, proving an incitement.

'You've only just walked in the door. I'll get it for you,' and she hurried to the oven, peeled the silver foil from the plate and carried it to the table.

'It's bloody dried up,' he roared. 'Do you really expect me to eat that? I want a decent meal when I get home after a hard day's work. Is that too much to ask?'

'We always eat at seven, Brett.' Hs wife tried to sound as reasonable as possible. Reason might be placating, but argument wasn't the answer for someone spoiling for a fight.

Troy could tell she was frightened. He heard the resounding crack of the slap across his mother's face.

At this point in the story, Troy stopped the flow of words that had been coming like a haemorrhage, and looked at the floor, wrestling for composure before he resumed. That slap was as immediate for him then as it had been the night before. Michael later wondered how many times he had relived that moment in the last eighteen hours, heard the slap like a rifle shot, seen the startled look on his mother's face? How many times would he continue to do so? Had it already punctured the tender fabric of his sleep, woken him with a start?

His mother didn't move, not daring to speak or retreat, not even raising her hands to her trembling face as the tears coursed down her cheeks.

Time stood still, waiting for the denouement. A pinkness was already blooming and deepening on her cheek.

Michael thought of the gentle woman downstairs who filled the room with serenity, and felt something close to hate for Brett Douglas bubble up within him. What sort of monster was Troy's father?

'That'll bloody teach you to be smart and answer back,' his father growled. The violence of the assault brought no self-reproach. 'Stop blubbering, woman,' he warned, but his mother couldn't, and almost choked trying to do so.

'I couldn't help it,' Troy told Michael. 'If I'd stopped and thought about it…' but he didn't finish the sentence. 'It was so unfair, so cruel. I charged at him. I don't know what I had in mind. He'd really hurt Mum. I just wanted it all to stop, to go away. But I didn't get a chance to do him any damage even if I'd planned to.'

Michael imagined the towering picture of the hefty Mr Douglas he'd seen in Troy's room, and watched his friend, pale and slight, even diminished by the telling of his story.

Troy was thrown backwards by the blow that landed on the side of his face. This time it was with a closed fist. It felt as if his head was about to explode. He tried to move his jaw, fearing it was broken, and lay on the floor, senseless for a few seconds before his father started cursing. This time, Troy reported, with the 'f' word.

'I'll teach you to meddle,' his father shouted. 'You're just like your mother,' and he made his way towards Troy, who had already scrambled to his feet, wide-eyed with alarm, and started to run. His father lumbered behind, removing the heavy studded belt from his trousers. The air was stinking of alcohol.

Troy was terrified, and could hear his mother screaming, imploring and panting heavily to find breath as his father advanced.

'No, Brett. No. No.' She sank to her knees, both hands to her head, but never stopped watching her son with horror-stricken eyes.

A knock on the bedroom door interrupting Troy's story was timely, as he was becoming more agitated.

'Are you two boys all right in there?' Mrs Douglas called from behind the door.

'Yes, Mum,' Troy answered, the interruption serving to slow the escalating flood of emotion.

'Are you sure I can't get you something? Another biscuit, Michael?'

'No thank you, Mrs Douglas,' Michael answered. 'Oh, and Mrs Douglas…'

'Yes, Michael?' She paused at the door.

'I think you're terrific.' Suddenly he was embarrassed. Why say that?

'Why, thank you, Michael,' she said curiously.

Michael later realised that she must have known Troy was telling him what had happened, and was reaching out to both of them.

When the boys heard her footsteps on the stairs, Troy continued. It was a cold winter's day, and the earlier sun was bluffed by cloud, dulling the room.

'I headed for the stairs,' Troy resumed. 'There was nowhere else to go. The front door was closed and I wouldn't have had time to open it before my father struck. My bedroom was at the top of the stairs, not that it would offer much relief. It could only delay the inevitable. I wasn't thinking. There was nowhere to hide anyway.'

He cleared the first three stairs in one jump and heard his father fall, with another volley of curses. A hand brushed his leg. He could feel its roughness, smell the heat and stink of his father's breath. The removal of his belt, dangling from his right hand like a deadly mace, had caused his trousers to gather around his ankles and trip him.

Troy raced into his bedroom and closed the door, expecting his father any second. The door couldn't be locked, so it was only temporary relief, a few seconds' reprieve at best. And it wouldn't have been the first time his father had splintered a door or gyprock wall with his fist or a heavy boot. Troy was terrified as he ran to the walk-in robe, the only space that could afford any protection, and concealed himself as best he could behind his clothes, closing the door.

Michael looked towards the walk-in robe and tried to imagine what it was like behind the closed doors. It was the first place someone would look, and a nine-year-old boy could easily be dragged into the open. Troy's bed mattress was on top of pull-out drawers and didn't offer a hiding place underneath.

'Michael.' Troy stopped the account. 'I'll never tell anyone this as long as I live, but I know I can trust you, but you must promise…that you'll never…'

'I promise, Troy,' Michael said. 'Your secrets will always be safe with me,' and his next admission was for Michael, at that stage in his life, the most poignant of all.

'I wet myself,' Troy said with his eyes lowered.

Michael didn't know what to say, unschooled as he was at that age to deal with another's pain. Such an accident was a source of great shame for a nine-year-old. He'd never forget the sniggers when Jennifer Bell had to be excused in second class after an accident she tried to conceal with Miss Brodie's help, and how she was embarrassed for weeks as much by the sympathy as the taunting.

After half a minute of silence, Troy continued. 'I don't know how long I stayed in the wardrobe. It might have been a couple of hours. I started by kneeling because it made me look smaller, harder to identify, but I soon cramped and had to stretch my legs. My cheek was throbbing and I could feel the skin pinching and drawing like a curtain around my eye. I didn't know if the wetness was water or blood, and couldn't see in the dark. Once, I touched my face with my finger and tried to identify the taste. It didn't taste like blood. With every little noise, a creaking of floorboards or a settling in the walls, I thought he was coming, but I guess he went back to eat what he could of his dinner. The shouting subsided after a while but I dared not get out of the wardrobe, even though the smell of naphthalene was making me sick.'

Michael tried to imagine what it must have been like for Troy. He hadn't been afraid of the dark, but he recalled being in an underground cave at the end of a long tunnel with his father when his flashlight stopped working. It was black with no visibility at all, no cues to give a sense of direction, and he was afraid. Luckily, his father was able to retrace their steps. And for Troy, the door could have been rent open at any moment to frame the towering and vengeful figure of his father.

After a long while, Troy could hear them in their bedroom next door to his. The bed was jumping noisily on the floor every second or two, the mattress was squeaking, and his mother was calling out and crying.

'You're hurting me, Brett. Please stop. No, no!'

'I couldn't hear what he was saying.' Troy seemed really distressed, knowing that his mother was suffering great indignities. 'It was more like a low growl. It all stopped suddenly, and there was silence. When it had been quiet for some time, I crept out. I didn't want to wake him and remind him of my escape. I took off my wet shorts that had begun to stink, but wasn't game to go to the bathroom to wash them. My bedside clock said twelve o'clock when I went to bed, but I couldn't sleep.'

It was to become a familiar scenario for the mornings after.

Troy's father did apologise to him, but downplayed the seriousness of what he had done, assuming a false cheer, even a jocularity. 'Sorry about hitting you, Troy,' he said, as though it were some minor transgression. 'Lost my cool for a moment there.' He didn't say anything about hitting Mrs Douglas. Perhaps what happened in the bedroom the night before was his warped gesture of apology to her, a peace offering of sorts.

Troy's mother kept watching him throughout the family's silent breakfast, wanting to treat his swollen cheek and his closed and weeping eye, but not wanting to draw her husband's attention to what he had done.

'Better tell them at school you walked into a door,' his father said. 'High five, mate,' he said light heartedly, holding up the palm of his hand in salute.

Troy half-raised his arm so that his father had to stoop to make contact. And, kissing his wife with a hurried peck, he left for work.

Even at the tender age of nine, it didn't escape Troy's understanding that his father was feeling some guilt, if not genuine remorse, but trying to diminish the significance of what had happened with false cheer. It was obvious that he was anxious to escape the house, and the scene of his abusing as soon as possible. As far as he was concerned, time would be the great healer. Heartfelt apology ran a poor second. It wasn't manly.

'Why couldn't he apologise as if he really meant it?' Troy asked his mother. 'Will it ever be any different?'

Michael wondered if it wasn't the first time, and whether it wouldn't be the last. He tried to make a child's sense of the family photograph on the bedside table, the gentle smiling mother and the grinning amiable father who could transform himself into a villain of terrifying and bearlike menace. And Troy was the buffer between them. It was a valuable lesson they didn't teach at school. People are not always the same.

'He really can be very kin,d Troy.' His mother, ever loyal, felt the need to defend her husband, and after she'd swabbed his cheek and applied ointment, she held Troy in a long embrace. Her cheeks were wet.

It wasn't the last time. There were a few occasions in Troy's primary and secondary school years when he was unusually sullen and uncommunicative. He didn't have any apparent injuries, though sometimes he'd favour a shoulder or walk gingerly.

The teachers often accused him of not trying hard enough, condemning his lethargy in class, but he had so much natural ability that he managed to scrape through, even if he did underachieve.

He was serious about observing his pact with Michael of sharing their feelings, and mentioned a few instances of his father being abusive when he'd been drinking, but he wasn't forthcoming with details. At least he'd gone partway in observing the contract. Michael didn't pry. Troy would talk if he needed to.

'Has your mum ever thought about leaving him,' Michael asked when Troy did want to talk, 'and taking you with her?'

Troy was silent for a while. It was a very adult question. Home was all they knew in those tender years, and he was fearful of losing such a foundation, even if the bedrock was crumbling. 'She's never mentioned it,' he answered.

In their first year of secondary school, Troy's father took them to Manly, where they stayed in a hotel.

'After everything I've told you, I won't blame you if you don't want to go,' Troy said apologetically, 'but he insists on taking me, and wants me to bring a friend. I think it's his way of apologising.'

Michael was excited. He wanted to go, and knew that Troy would be anxious, and possibly more of a target if he were left alone with his father. He hadn't been worried about suffering abuse at the hands of Troy's father, but was surprised by his generosity and concern. Mr Douglas took them to the beach and the aquarium, and paid for all their meals. He was equally attentive to both boys, swam with them in the surf, and joined with them in runs along the beach. While Michael never doubted that his friend had suffered abuse, he began to wonder if Troy's accounts of that abuse were exaggerated. He knew that people could change, but Mr Douglas seemed so considerate.

Troy could see what he was thinking, and it must have saddened him. But he didn't say anything.

'Mum was sitting in the passenger seat of a police car when I got there, staring straight ahead. It wasn't that her look said something in particular that spooked me…like pain, shock, disbelief…it said nothing, nothing at all. Her face was a mask, a blank mask. She'd collapsed when she arrived back home and they told her. There was a police officer, a woman, sitting in the driver's seat next to her. She was on the police radio. Mum, I said, and she didn't answer. Mum, I said more loudly, and she still kept looking ahead without saying a thing. I'll never forget that look…it was so scary. Another policeman was gentle with me, trying to shield me from the details, but I wanted to know. So he pointed to the upstairs window where my father fell. He'd been mumbling something about having to fix the eaves before I left for uni. So I walked with the policeman to where he landed. There was blood on the sandstone edging of the garden, and more on the grass. Real dark it was. Mrs Russell, the ironing woman, found him, and I can just imagine what her reaction must have been. She'd be telling her friends for months. I suppose it was a small mercy that his body had been taken away before my mother got back from her midweek tennis. There was no way of knowing when it happened.'

'What was it like,' Michael asked, 'seeing where it happened?' wondering if he sounded ghoulish, but Troy didn't mind. They were used to asking things that respectability would prevent others from asking. And Troy needed to talk.

'It was strange,' Troy answered. 'That feeling of being there, and somewhere else…the feeling that it's not happening to you, but you're standing outside it all looking in.'

Troy stopped for a moment before continuing. 'Strange too that it was this man I'd been frightened of for all those years…and I kept imagining how he must have looked, crumpled in a heap near the flower bed.'

Troy had been with Michael at the university when they received the news. They were both eighteen. Troy was studying environmental science, and Michael was studying to be a teacher. He had offered to skip classes and support Troy in returning home, but Troy thought it best that he be alone with his mother.

The funeral was well attended, and Brett was eulogised for his consideration and sense of humour. He was praised as a conscientious worker, and a devoted husband and father. Troy remained expressionless throughout with his head bowed. Mrs Douglas dabbed at her eyes with a sodden tissue and held Troy's hand as if her life depended on it.

Troy qualified for university accommodation shortly after that, and Michael made frequent visits to his basic room in a complex of four. He made new friends. His mother moved away. She remarried soon afterwards.

'In spite of everything,' Troy said to Michael, visibly upset, 'I did love him, you know.'

'She was my saviour,' Michael remembered Troy telling him, and he wasn't surprised. They weren't alike, but they might have complemented each other. It wasn't just that Stephanie was assured and outgoing, and Troy more withdrawn and even introspective. She brought a balance and a sanity to the relationship to counter Troy's lack of certainty and cynicism. 'My saviour' he'd called her, and he did need rescuing.

Since the relationship began, Michael had noticed a change in his friend. He seemed happier. He was embracing life, showing more of an interest in people and what was happening around him. Michael felt that he had a new friend, the old friend with the good magnified, and the less attractive diminished. He'd long ago given up trying to explain what attracted people to each other, believing that such a dynamic defies analysis, and is even beyond the powers of the couple involved.

He wanted to believe that the change was permanent, that Troy wouldn't retreat as love mellowed. And he wanted to believe that

Stephanie knew what she was letting herself in for. Troy would certainly have revealed to her his history of abuse, and he knew Stephanie to be nurturing.

There was nothing remarkable about their courtship. There were no fierce separations and no passionate reunions. Michael saw the evenness of their relationship as a useful recruiting of each other to a shared vision of reality.

It was a church wedding, and the reception was held at a grand old mansion with a huge dining room, a ballroom and vaulted ceilings. The bridesmaids wore apple green, and the groomsmen wore black tuxedos with white carnations. A demure Beth Douglas couldn't stop smiling.

Michael was Troy's best man, and Tiffany was invited, though not as a bridesmaid. Michael had to plead with her to go.

'But I won't be sitting with you,' she said. 'I'll be with people I don't know, and you'll be on the official table.'

She did make an effort, though, and looked particularly attractive. He'd never seen her dressed formally before.

Michael's speech avoided the usual pabulum of wedding speeches, but was full of humour. Troy's speech was softly spoken and measured. Beth thought of how Brett would have revelled in the opportunity to make a speech. He'd have been so proud.

As they ran or walked the gauntlet of their guests to the streamer-decked car with its 'just married' signs, Stephanie hugged Michael and kissed his cheek, leaving a faint hint of lipstick.

'I'm so happy,' she whispered, her eyes alight. He could feel her glow beneath the cotton of her going-away dress, and the thump of her heart, a message between them.

'Thank you for everything,' Troy said, shaking his hand. 'I mean, for always being there,' and then, more cryptically, 'everything's as it should be, isn't it?'

4

Michael couldn't see Tiffany sitting at the back of the church at Troy and Stephanie's wedding because, as best man, he was standing beside Troy as the priest married them. While it wasn't the real reason for wanting Tiffany to be at the wedding, it had occurred to him that watching another couple exchanging vows could do his own cause of furthering their relationship no harm. It might, it just might plant a seed for the future.

It had been years since Tiffany had been to church. She sat at the end of a pew near a side wall feeling overwhelmed. There was something ethereal, something beyond life here. She felt a presence, a sense of moving spirit, but whether it was her own or something else, she couldn't tell.

She raised her eyes to the high vaulted roof supported by massive oak beams. Beside her, Mary and the infant Jesus in bright colours were immobilised in swirls of lead and stained glass, translucent and luminous from the sun outside. Gold shone from the altar and from an ornately carved eagle fronting the pulpit.

She was roused by the grandness of the organ as Pachelbel's Canon announced the entry of the bridesmaids. Heads turned and moved forwards and backwards to peer around others and see. Tiffany's didn't. There were admiring noises as Stephanie entered.

Michael couldn't see Tiffany's tears as Troy and Stephanie exchanged the vows they'd written themselves. Both vows were testament to the love they felt and the certainty of a happy future. Michael searched his pocket for the ring, came up empty handed and gave a helpless shrug. The guests were open-mouthed, but he quickly revealed it in his other hand. Troy smiled. He knew his friend well.

As soon as he was able, Michael left the bridal table to dance with

Tiffany. A few young couples were dancing in locked embrace, kissing as they shuffled on the spot. Older couples held each other more discreetly, reliving fond memories. Tiffany was warm with Michael but not inclined to similar intimacy.

They'd been doing more together in the last month, and were seen by Michael's close friends as a couple. Michael couldn't see enough of her and, to his great satisfaction, Tiffany was sometimes taking the lead. His greatest pleasure was seeing her laugh, but there were other moments too, natural moments like her stooping to pat a dog and chatting with the owners, insisting on buying ice creams and tasting some of his, and walking along the beach ankle-deep in water with her jeans rolled up.

She resisted going away together, and if they returned to her place at the end of a day, as they often did, their relationship closed in on itself, its shine and promise disappearing with the sun.

One day, they went to Lake Parramatta, a picturesque place where a deep olive-green lake is surrounded by tall gums, many of them clawing their footing into a rocky foreshore. There are grassy areas, picnic tables and a small kiosk.

As they entered the kiosk for morning coffee, an odd-looking woman wheeling her tiny luggage to a small table in the corner called to the waiter, 'So has he been today?'

'Not today, Grace. Perhaps tomorrow.'

Grace, a woman of indeterminate years with a heavily wrinkled face and slight stoop, didn't order. They placed her in her late sixties or early seventies. She had greying hair that must have been raven in earlier years, and wore a shapeless floral skirt, a white blouse, floppy hat and track shoes. She sat staring across the lake waiting for her regulation order. An assortment of coins was scattered on the table.

An hour later, they saw her again sitting near the water's edge, looking across the sunlit olive of the lake, watching the ducks in gleaming phalanx and the sulphur-crested cockatoos playing tag between the towering gum trees.

She rose quickly to her feet when she saw them approach. 'Have you seen a man,' she said, 'grey eyes and very regal, about so high,' and she motioned with a benedictory hand, 'possibly in khaki slacks and a mustard top?'

'No, sorry,' Michael replied.

Tiffany shook her head.

She sat down with no apparent disappointment, and they watched her accosting every passer-by with the same enquiry.

'Have you seen a man, grey eyes? He might be wearing khaki slacks and a mustard top.'

Returning to the kiosk for lunch, they asked the waiter about Grace.

'We call her "mad Grace",' he said. 'No disrespect. She hasn't missed a day here in well over thirty years. And always here, the same old floppy hat, the umbrella all skew-whiff with broken spokes, and wheeling her odds and ends.' He paused. 'I guess some feelings can't be numbed by time. To keep believing blunts the loneliness.'

'Tomorrow,' Grace called, and all eyes turned to watch her shambling gait, and time stood still until the squeaking wheels were heard no more and silence for a moment overwhelmed.

'I've been thinking about that woman,' Tiffany said a few days later. 'There must be something we can do for her.'

So they returned to the lake and found Grace sitting by the foreshore where she'd accosted them before.

'Could you tell me,' she said as they approached, 'if you've seen a man, about so tall, grey eyes, very distinguished looking, khaki trousers and mustard top?'

'Can you tell me his name?' Tiffany said gently.

'You've seen him.' Grace was suddenly alert.

'No, no,' Tiffany was quick not to raise her hopes. 'It might help a little if people had more information to go on…a name or detailed description.'

Grace was happy to share what she knew, which wasn't much. They'd only met once, and his name was Alan. She told them of that meeting with a far-away look in her eyes.

Tiffany was determined to help mad Grace find her lost love. 'We must,' she said to Michael, 'before…well, before it's too late.'

She wasn't daunted by having nothing to go on, so she and Michael spent two full days enquiring at local shops, catching people in the front yards of nearby homes, and approaching businesses and other organisations in the district. It was a tall order. Very few people could boast thirty years in the same home or organisation.

Michael was proud of Tiffany. He'd rarely seen her so committed. It had become a crusade.

'We tried,' Michael consoled her. 'That's the important thing. For all we know, Alan might not have been his real name anyway. She might have forgotten it, or he might have had good reason not to tell her.'

Rather than giving comfort, Michael's words irritated Tiffany.

As the word spread, well-meaning people were keen to share their information. They received several phone calls, having left their numbers with the kiosk proprietor. Two calls were from wives whose husbands had decamped with younger women.

They had all but given up when a call came from a woman whose husband was in a nearby nursing home. One of the occupants was Alan Lodge, late sixties, tall with grey eyes.

The nursing home was happy to let Michael, after being suitably vetted, take a resident for a brief outing. Tiffany made the plan. Michael would take Alan for morning tea to a nearby café while she would stay at the nursing home and try to find out what she could about Alan's history.

His room was one of many off a stone-coloured linoleum corridor. It had a single bed, a wardrobe and a small writing desk. Two nondescript abstract prints hung from the wall. The room was sombre, though sunlight was trying to squeeze through shuttered slats. A porcelain vase of orange gerberas was wilting on the sill.

He was the right age and his eyes were grey. He was apprehensive to see them, but they'd been well-briefed and told not to expect too much. They imagined him swaddled in his bed, his only immunity from anxiety, and his only comfort in the things he knew, the elaborate cornices and frosted ceiling light, the door that opened on his wandering thoughts to capture muted voices from adjacent rooms, the cheery appearance of the nurse at eight a.m. with pills and prophylactic words.

Michael helped him into an old maroon cardigan from his wardrobe, and they set off. The day was picturebook blue and warm. But the storm was his. They'd only gone a hundred metres when the clouds were louring for him, catching him in indecision's parody. He moved a step forward, looked anxiously around, took a step backwards looking stricken, and turned, taking no heed of Michael, hurrying back to the nursing home. Michael had no option but to follow. Why force challenges he dared not face?

'Alan,' the nursing sister held Michael's look and shrugged. 'Are you sure, Alan. It's such a lovely day.'

So the planned morning tea became gin rummy with the three of them in a room that was shrinking with him, and with stewed tea and ginger snaps. Alan was silent throughout, yet showed a flicker of pleasure when told that he had won.

They left after an hour, knowing that he'd listen to their departing steps tick tock receding along the linoleum corridor to fade into welcome silence.

'I found a letter,' Tiffany said, waving it in the air as they climbed into their car.

'Tiffany,' Michael protested. 'It's not yours to take!'

'We can always send it back,' she answered with a mischievous smile. 'Do you really think he's going to miss it?'

She opened the letter and read it aloud as they sat in the car.

My dear Grace,

I hope you don't mind me using the possessive 'my', and after having only met once. Yesterday was the most wonderful, and at the same time the most terrible day of my life.

It was the most wonderful because I met you. I have recalled every word we spoke, every one of the looks I read on your face.

Have you ever felt so completely absorbed in someone, that nothing else seems real, as if the rest of the world is tapping on the window pane of your being trying to get in, and can't? I hadn't.

Remember I said that my divorce was to be finalised in a couple of weeks. Well, when I arrived home from seeing you, my wife reported that she had a particularly aggressive cancer. True, because she showed me the medical report.

I know I said we'd meet tomorrow (same place, same time) but I hope you'll understand if I can't be there. She's not handling it at all well! Things may be very unsettled for a while, and I have to give my support.

You know you're where my heart is. Is it silly to say I'm missing you when less than a day has passed? I'll try to get someone to take this letter to the man at the kiosk to pass on to you.

Love, Alan.

The letter, still unposted, was continued twenty-nine days later and related his wife's death, its impact upon him, his dreams of her, and concluded a fortnight later with:

Haven't sent these ramblings yet. Sorry. I feel very down. A real mix of warring emotions.

Do you still care, Grace? Did that day at the lake really happen? Or am I imagining it, reading too much into it? Was it a fleeting need in a passing moment in each of our lives that propelled us together?

Tiffany had begun to cry almost as soon as she started to read, and had to stop a couple of times before sniffling and continuing. 'Well, it's certainly our Alan,' she said, refolding the letter carefully as though it were precious.

The following day, they sat in the kiosk having morning tea. It was another luminous day of sun-drenched blue. A flock of sulphur-crested cockatoos flew from tree to tree screeching. They could see Grace sitting some eighty metres away in the second spot she'd claimed as her own by the foreshore.

A couple passed, and she rose to her feet. She raised her hand, no doubt demonstrating the height of a man in khaki slacks and mustard top.

Michael and Tiffany had come wondering what to tell her. They hadn't agreed on a way forward.

Michael was uneasy about telling her anything of what they'd discovered. 'I don't think it would be kind to do so,' he reflected. 'I think Alan's whereabouts should remain a secret.'

'You can't be serious.' Tiffany was annoyed. She was implacable. 'She has every right to know. Why do we have the right to play God?'

'But we weren't prepared for how we'd find him.' Michael was less certain, but firming in his opposition. 'He probably won't have any idea who she is. And you'd have to admit that Grace is not fully with it herself. And even if she does recognise him, there's her disappointment to consider. It could crush her.'

'They loved each other, Michael. I really think you don't understand.' Tiffany was annoyed. 'And they probably still do love each other. Just because he's only half there, doesn't mean…doesn't mean…at least he's there.' She was near tears.

'You don't think it's better that she preserve a meaningful fantasy than indulge a suspect reality?' Michael was trying to consider what it meant for both of them.

'No, I certainly do not!'

'Bye,' Grace interrupted them cheerily. 'Tomorrow, then.'

Their eyes turned to watch her retreat, as the sound of squeaking wheels faded to silence.

Michael used to have night dreams as a child, mainly about being punished at school by Mrs Rouse. Sometimes it was tigers. But since meeting Tiffany, the dreaming had returned. He had a dream the night after the wedding that made him wake with a start in a cold sweat.

He was in heated disagreement with a man over something, though it wasn't clear what that something was. He would pull it in his direction claiming ownership, and the man, dark and surly, would argue that it was his, and pull it away.

'It's mine,' Michael, at first quietly reasonable, would begin to shout.

'It was bloody well mine before it was yours,' the man screamed and grabbed at it with one hand, pushing Michael away with the other.

They stopped tugging and set to fighting, grappling, throwing punches, rolling in the dirt and trying to pull the other's hair.

The man was the first to rise, covered in dirt and with a bloodied ear. He was holding a sword. It had a long shiny blade that winked silver in the broad daylight sun.

'I can settle this once and for all,' he snarled, and came at Michael with the sword raised in both hands above his head as though he was going to cleave Michael's head in two halves.

Michael dodged, turned and ran. The man followed. He was waving the sword as if he was having practice swipes. His face was a mask of hate.

Michael ran for kilometres. He ran for days. The man didn't give up. He was grimly determined.

Michael fell, tripping on a raised section of pavement. One knee was bloodied and his heart was thumping in his chest. The man, never far away, was getting closer.

'What do you want?' Michael yelled. 'What do you bloody want?'

The man didn't answer and kept coming. Michael hobbled as fast as he could. I'm dead he said to himself.

He ran into a town and through the main street. It was busy with cars. The streets were crowded. People were going about their business.

'Behind me, that man with the sword,' Michael panted, his chest aching. 'He's going to kill me.'

But the people he passed were indifferent.

'Excuse me.' He stopped momentarily, addressing a man in some sort of official uniform. 'Can you help me? A man is trying to kill me.'

But the official didn't seem to hear him. Or see him.

He was exhausted, and the man kept coming. He was close enough now for Michael to see the look of satisfaction on the man's face. The chase was nearing an end. He was coming in for the kill.

In a panic, Michael turned abruptly into a narrow alleyway, hoping to lose his pursuer. It was dark, and buildings rose tall on both sides shutting out the sun.

It didn't take long to realise his mistake. The alley ended with a brick wall. The alley itself was only a hundred metres long. He'd come to a dead end. There was no way out except for the way he'd come in. He turned to face the street, wondering as he did so whether his pursuer had lost the scent.

But standing at the entrance in the half-light, there were not one, but two figures, barely discernible, standing side by side. It suddenly felt bitterly cold. He could see the glint of something silver.

He was surprised and pleased when Margaret Thurgood called and invited him to afternoon tea. She had extended her stay with Tiffany. He wasn't sure if Tiffany would be there or not. If she was, so much the better. If not, Margaret was excellent company, and he might very well learn something about Tiffany.

They drank coffee and ate scones with jam and cream, before Margaret brought out the photo album.

'Don't worry,' she laughed. 'When people wade through the family photos, you lose the will to live. I'll only show you a few.'

There were two of Tiffany as a young girl dressed for sport and holding a hockey stick. She had white spindly legs, was freckled and squinting in the sun. Another showed her in late adolescence dressed in a snug-fitting gown. Her womanly figure was apparent.

'School graduation,' Margaret told him.

She was sitting next to him on the lounge, turning the pages. He could feel her warmth.

He felt a little sad. Photos of loved ones always left him with a sense of vanquished time, the flow of years and the separateness of lives.

The next photo was of Tiffany and Paul. He had the feeling that its appearance at this point was strategic.

'That's Paul,' she said casually, as if he might not know.

They were standing side by side in the photo. Their arms were around each other. They were smiling. Michael knew that Margaret was watching him.

'You love her, don't you, Michael?' The question was put so naturally, and with such tender feeling, it didn't seem presumptuous.

He didn't have a problem saying yes and, having answered, began to think about what he really felt. Was it real love when it existed somewhere in the space between yearning and fulfilment? And if it wasn't, what was it? He felt he could talk to Margaret. He liked her. But just how much do you reveal to a mother?

'Of course you know about Paul,' she said. 'I think I'm in the same position as you,' she smiled, 'wondering how much to say.' She paused. 'I could say you need to be very gentle with Tiffany at the moment. She's still going through a difficult time. But I think you know that.'

'Margaret,' he said, feeling confident in taking her hand, 'I think we both know where each of us is at, and what the other is thinking.'

'I think we do, Mr Manton,' and her laugh rescued them both from becoming maudlin.

5

'It felt really strange, like I didn't belong.' Troy had just returned from visiting his mother. They had kept in touch by phone, but this had been his first visit. 'I'd never thought about names before, how important they are,' he reflected. 'They define us. They give us identity.'

'But she's still Mrs Douglas,' Michael said.

They were sitting together in the small café in Epping that had become their usual monthly meeting place. They used to swap memories of lost and desired loves. Most were fictions, but there was no delusion. It was part of their mythology. But since Troy's marriage, their conversation covered different topics.

It was always the same, a large flat white for Troy and a mocha for Michael. They shared a raisin toast.

'No, that's just it,' Troy replied, looking disappointed. 'She's now Mrs Pithers. Can you believe that? Mrs Adrian Pithers. When I heard it, I felt like a big hand had lifted me up and plonked me down somewhere else. I know she still loves me, I know I'm still a part of her life, but I felt…well, I felt…kind of…dispossessed.'

'Surely what matters, Troy, is that she does still love you.'

'Don't get me wrong. I'm really pleased for her. And I'm not jealous. At least I don't think I am. Adrian, Adrian Pithers, seems like a really nice bloke, tall, shock of thinning white hair and a gentle manner. They couldn't have made me more welcome. He acted more like a mate than a father.'

'But Troy, you're an adult now, a married man.' Michael was surprised. 'How should he have behaved?'

'Yeah, I suppose.' Troy was reliving the experience of his visit. 'Just walking around the house, seeing the bedroom, the double bed where they slept together, the big kitchen with everything that opens and shuts, the study with a leather inset desk and Adrian's display of World War I model soldiers and memorabilia.

'Your room,' and he showed me a room…I could see my mother's hand at work… 'when you come to stay.'

'Everything does move on.' Michael hoped he didn't sound trite. 'And your mother must be so much happier now.'

'Oh, and they have a dog, a golden retriever. I always wanted a dog.'

Michael had been shown a recent photo of Troy, a candid Instamatic shot of four fellows carousing at a barbecue with steins raised high in mock salute, a shot that lopped a waving hand and reddened eyes like feral cats. A grinning male was standing in the foreground and seemed to be conducting a singing fest with tongs between turning meat. Troy was one of them, standing in the background and not singing. His eyes looked dark and brooding. There were no women. The picture left Michael wondering.

'So how's married life?' Michael asked when Troy had finished talking about his visit.

'Good.'

'Good. Is that all?'

'Great, then.' Troy was suddenly testy. 'What do you want me to say?'

Michael was silent. He wasn't going to be provocative, though Troy's answer did seem lukewarm.

'Sorry. Everyone asks me that, as if being married leads to some great dramatic change, makes you into something you never were.'

'Well, doesn't it?'

'I can't find any fault with Stephanie,' Troy answered, dodging the question. 'She's an angel.' He nodded to himself as if affirming a realised truth, but said no more.

'You're a lucky man,' and Michael stood to leave, patting Troy's shoulder.

Michael chanced upon Stephanie in the supermarket. They hugged, pleased to see each other. It was an excuse to have coffee together.

'How are things with Tiffany?' she asked as they sat down and ordered.

Michael drew breath before he answered. He couldn't fool Stephanie. 'A work in progress,' he said.

'Aren't they all?' Stephanie replied, and laughed. She knew better than to pursue the matter. It wasn't just Michael's hesitation and guarded answer. She had witnessed Tiffany's restraint towards him. She had seen his eagerness to please, and the tension between them that was sometimes palpable. She knew Michael well and was concerned for him.

'And Troy?' Michael asked.

Stephanie's face clouded. 'I've been wanting to ask you, Michael.' She was suddenly serious. 'I know men don't talk much to each other about these things, but has Troy ever said anything to you about his feelings…for me, I mean.'

'Only the other day, Steph, he told me you were an angel.'

'That's something,' she answered and, after a moment's reflection, 'but is that a label that might be used without feeling? If I call you a saint, does that say anything about my feelings for you? Or is it like saying so-and-so is a great swimmer, a superb cook, a good artist? Where is the emotion? Is it hiding somewhere, perhaps behind the protective intellect, or doesn't it exist at all?' She shook her head. 'Perhaps I'm just being silly.' Stephanie was getting upset. Her question was more than idle interest.

'I'm quite sure Troy loves you, every bit as much as it's possible for a man to love a woman.'

'Or perhaps every bit as much as it's possible for Troy to love a woman.'

Michael had no answer, or at least none that he wanted to share. This was no mere tit for tat. Stephanie might be right.

'I've had boyfriends before, as you well know, Michael Manton.' She smiled. Her composure had returned, though a tear had gathered, a crystal on an eyelash. She took his hand and squeezed it. 'Most of them spoke of love, and I only had to look in their faces to see it. It's different with Troy.'

He tried to reassure her with the usual take on gender differences, but even as he spoke, he knew it sounded hollow.

When Stephanie had gone, Michael recalled the photo of the men at the barbecue, and Troy's cryptic and matter-of-fact assessment of his wedding day. What was it again? He had to think. 'Everything's as it should be,' he'd said. Of all the wild, passionate, abandoned things a man might say on the day his love is sanctified, his dream realised, he falls back on what is appropriate, what it should be.

But was it that unusual, he kept thinking. Surely there are some people, men and women, for whom love will always be circumscribed, people who will always keep something in reserve, a cache for rainy days that will never come, people who are desperate to give themselves to another and can't, people who want to love but who have a circumstantial will against it.

Wattamolla beach and picnic ground is a beautiful and isolated spot in the Royal National Park near Wollongong. A calm lagoon flows to the ocean and is ideal for swimming and snorkelling. Groves of cabbage tree palm offer protection from the sun and prying eyes, and there are several coastal bushwalks. There are no shops or kiosks nearby.

Michael and Tiffany had been to the beach together before, but they usually walked for kilometres along the water's edge, with Tiffany, her jeans rolled up, letting the gentle lapping waves roll over her ankles. It had been a cool beginning to spring.

This day was royal blue and hot, and they'd brought a picnic lunch of warm French bread, cabanossi, Camembert and a Greek salad. They lay on their towels in the sun. Michael, wearing black swimming costumes and a white towelling top, was pretending not to notice Tiffany's pale figure in a red bikini.

He had never seen her this undressed before. She was lying on her stomach with her head turned away, so he could look without her thinking him a voyeur. Respectability, though, was so ingrained in him, he still only allowed himself the occasional glance.

Much of how she looked was new to him. Her semi-nakedness gave form to the abstract, substance to the idea. The one slight blemish, a near-invisible two-centimetre scar on her hip, made her more real, something more authentic than the flawless ersatz images in glossy magazines. He was fascinated by the gradual swell of thighs from her knees, and the rise of her buttocks. He was aroused, and wondered if she knew he was.

Was her lying there in her costume an accident of the seasons, the arrival of hot weather, or was there some other purpose? Had she discreetly turned her head giving him the opportunity to look? No, he decided. He'd have been delighted if that were true, but she had always avoided the provocative in words, looks and actions. She was beyond such artifice.

'Come on, Michael,' she called, climbing to her feet, and reaching out to take his hand and pull him up, 'let's swim to that rock,' and she pointed to a large rock rising two metres from the sea and about fifty metres from the shore.

Michael cast off his reverie and rose to his feet, turning away from her in the hope that his arousal didn't show. They ran hand in hand to the water's edge and dived together, striking out towards the rock. Tiffany was a strong swimmer and reached the rock a few metres before him. They trod water for a minute, and he watched the water coursing down her face, her eyes agleam. He'd never seen her so alive.

'Race you back to shore,' she called. 'Ready, set,' and her 'go' came after she'd already taken several strokes.

She reached the shore before Michael, and seemed pleased. 'I've always lost that race,' she said, drying her hair.

Michael's mood darkened with those words, yet he said nothing. Tiffany didn't seem to notice.

She put on her cheesecloth top and beckoned to Michael to follow. They entered a grove of cabbage tree palms and explored, walking over fallen pods that crunched beneath their bare feet, leaving a treacle-coloured stain. They walked to the lagoon, watched teenage boys jumping from a high rock into the deep end, and dabbled at its edge in the warm brackish water. They didn't say much. The natural world seemed to put a brake on idle talk.

Tiffany seemed less restrained. She was quiet but not introspective. There were moments of real happiness. She slept in the car on the way home, her head against the side window.

When they reached her unit, there was a mist of rain, gentle and quiet as a blessing. The sky had turned a koala grey. They'd had the best of the day. He felt strangely satisfied, as though he was returning to home and hearth after an adventure together. Yes, 'together' was the operative word.

It was still warm inside, the west-facing windows heated by the afternoon sun. The familiarity of the place was pleasing. He'd always put his wallet and keys in the same place on the little table, taken the liberty of boiling the kettle for tea as soon as they arrived, sat on the same side of the lounge, the little rituals that relationships exact.

'You have the first shower,' he said as they'd entered.

They'd already agreed that he would stay for dinner. He hoped for longer. Her relaxed manner at Wattamolla had left him with a sense that this evening might be different.

'I'll get the takeaway,' he called after her. She'd already dropped her things on the floor, and was heading for the bathroom. 'The usual?'

'Let's try the beef and black bean,' she called back.

He had to wait at the Chinese restaurant. A lot of people had the same idea. The rain had stopped and there was a freshness and tang of pine in the air. Raindrops clung to leaves, bloating before they fell. The sky was a darkening mauve with threads of pink. Dusk brought a freedom, the mental liberty he felt when it was neither night nor day.

When he returned, she was fully dressed in loose linen slacks of sunflower yellow, and a white cotton top. A towel was wound around her drying hair. Her face was pink from the heat of the shower, and the sun had caught her nose. She'd run to the door when he'd rung. He didn't have a key. She was breathing heavily and her breasts were straining against her cotton blouse.

The plates, forks and serviettes were already on the coffee table. Dinners were always informal, sometimes in front of the television. He dished out the food and they ate in silence, she with chopsticks and he with a fork. It was dark, and the moon kept nudging its way between restless clouds.

'Good?' he asked after several minutes.

'Mmm,' she answered, wiping black bean sauce from her mouth.

He felt the beginnings of anxiety, the tightening in his chest. She was never very talkative, but after the day they'd just shared, he was hoping…

'You beat me in the race,' he said, hoping it might resurrect the day's pleasure.

'Yes.'

'By the proverbial mile,' he continued, and realised he was trying too hard. If she wanted to talk, she would. She didn't.

They finished the meal in silence.

'That was good,' he said. 'I tried the new place, the one on the corner with all the rose-coloured lights, the Golden something.' He was talking too much.

'Lantern.'

'Yes, lantern,' he mumbled, taking the plates to the kitchen. His exhilaration had left him.

He came back and sat in his usual place on the lounge. She was sitting at the other end, and made no move to bridge the gap. He wanted to be close to her, but felt unable to make the move.

As the silence continued, it became harder for them both to puncture it with words. His mind played with things he could say, but it was becoming impossible, an assault on silence. She seemed unmoved. It was a familiar scenario. How many times had he said a disappointed goodbye when he'd had reason to expect more? He was deflated.

He did consider a bold advance. A 'Come here, Thurgood', offered with a twinkle in the eyes, a beckoning smile as he'd take her in his arms. But even such a tactic, its motive disguised by light-heartedness, might be met with alarm. He'd be made to feel the assailant, inconsiderate and heartless,

'Well, I suppose I'd better be going.' He stood, waiting for a reaction. There was none.

'Yes,' she said softly. 'I suppose so.' She didn't move.

He headed slowly for the door.

'Michael.' Her call was peremptory, stopping him in his stride.

He turned, and she was against him, her arms wrapped around his back, pulling him to her, her lips open, full and wet, tasting faintly of black bean, pressed hard against his own. She was sliding her body up and down, rubbing herself against him, running her hands over his back. He could feel her tongue, a tooth as she gnawed at his lips. Had she yielded at last?

He was taken by surprise. The suddenness and the abandonment were beyond all hope. He was immediately aroused, prepared to be carried away by the flood.

She lifted his polo shirt, pulling it over his raised arms, to leave him bare from the waist, and reached down between their clasped bodies to grab at his sex. She was breathing heavily.

He was led hurriedly to the bedroom where she was undressed in seconds, only briefly standing marbled and lambent by the glow of the moon lodged in a windowpane, before she was impatiently tugging at his jeans. It was urgent for them both.

They fell on the bed together, their mouths locked, lying side by side. Nothing was said. It didn't have to be.

He was intoxicated by her taste and smell, and by the fullness and softness of her body. His hands explored. So did hers. He was hard, indomitable.

She rolled over, mounting, sitting astride him. He felt the exquisite pleasure of entering her, and watched her moving up and down, her eyes shut tight, her face in a slight frown, intent and intense.

The frenzied movement stopped suddenly as he came, a prodigious release, and she rolled away to lie on her back. She didn't move, and her eyes stayed closed.

He remained as she had left him, looking up at the ceiling. He felt sated, yet empty. It had been a whirlwind. What did it all mean? It should have made them one. It was the act by which people expressed their love, if there was any, so why did he feel so separate, and so desolate?

He knew she felt the same. She lay on her back, not having uttered a word, perfectly still. The last thing she'd said was her no-nonsense call of 'Michael'.

He wasn't sure how long they lay there. It could have been a few minutes or an hour. They didn't speak. He watched the branches of the tree near the window playing tricks with the moon on the bedroom ceiling, a scribble of images. He wondered if there was a message in the scribblings, a symbol, an irony. He began to feel cold. She remained still with her eyes shut.

When he closed his eyes for a few seconds, she rolled free of the bed. He saw the whiteness of her back and buttocks as she passed quickly into the living room.

He waited for several minutes, thinking she might return, thinking she might have something to say. But what? And what could he say to her? When it became apparent that she wouldn't come back, he dressed slowly and made his way from the bedroom. Would she be dressed, pretending like she had on that stormy night months ago, that nothing had happened?

He found her sitting forward on the lounge, staring ahead, dry-eyed, rocking backwards and forwards, holding the framed picture of herself and Paul against her naked breasts.

He sat in the car, heavy with tiredness, emotionally spent. It was black outside except for a bland disk of moon, pale-white and fathomless. He was haunted by the image of a near-demented Tiffany.

He felt like the first-time teenagers overwhelmed by lust in the back-seat of a car, lying with the aftermath, the trickle and glaze and bewilderment, searching the stars for answers, a collision of ships in the night…and no survivors.

What had it meant for Tiffany? That was obvious. The picture of her rocking backwards and forwards clinging on to the photo said it all. Sex in lieu, sex as analgesic to deaden the pain.

6

They sat at the table they'd claimed as their own on most Thursday nights for months. She was apprehensive and wooden at first. He began by disguising anxiety with a show of confidence.

He was surprised and relieved when she'd agreed to meet. His departing image of her the previous Saturday had proved indelible. When he'd slipped past her rocking on the lounge, clutching at the photo, she didn't seem to have noticed him go. He no longer existed. Was that a message, one that carried a terrible finality? Had his part in the action smashed the brittle porcelain of their relationship into a thousand fragments?

In his drive home that night, he'd even wondered if he still wanted to keep on seeing her. Her reaction had scared him. She was unhinged. These last months of searching for a sign of something normal in relationships had all been too much of a struggle. He was resigned to failure. Then he thought of what had happened that Saturday night, the sudden febrile collision between them, and thought it might have been a necessary evil, a smashing of restraints, a breaking of the bonds that held her back, that held them both back. Was it, with all its pain for her, a goodbye to Paul? Could the bewildering onslaught of lust now lead to a more loving consummation?

So he decided he still wanted to see her on Thursday night, and she'd reluctantly agreed. There was still the question of how to address what had happened. Should he ignore it, or tempt her with his glowing interpretation of what it all meant?

He couldn't resist mentioning it, trying to weave it seamlessly into the fabric of conversation, giving the impression that it was significant.

'I was thinking about the other night, Tiff,' he began.

'Don't read too much into it, Michael.' She was quick to answer. She had anticipated what was coming.

'I just wanted to say…'

'Can we leave it,' she said, though not unpleasantly.

The rest of the evening was no different from what it had always been, the usual questions and answers, surface talk. He was stung by her reaction, though it was not unexpected, and tried to remain upbeat.

She wasn't available for the next three Thursdays, and he was convinced he'd made the wrong decision. He should have ignored any mention of what had occurred. She must be annoyed. She hadn't called, and she hadn't answered his calls.

But she did finally call, asking him to accompany her to an art exhibition. Thank heavens for Deirdre, he thought. Deirdre, an old school friend, had two of her paintings hanging beside those of more established artists and wanted Tiffany to see them.

Michael was pleased. Perhaps this was a new beginning.

'You will come, Tiff,' Deirdre had pleaded, 'and bring that man of yours. I think you're hiding him from me.'

Her unit felt just the same when Michael went to pick her up. No sinister aura, though he did notice that the picture of Paul was no longer on the living room table.

It was a great relief to resume a normal, or near-normal, relationship. They made all the right noises standing in front of Deirdre's two paintings, a web of circles and lines in clashing colours that she described to them as humankind's search for meaning in an increasingly complex and technological world. When she left to enlighten other visitors, they looked at each other, and burst into laughter. It was a welcome moment for Michael, making them feel like conspirators.

For Michael, things were on the up and up. He dropped her at the door. For a second, they looked at each other awkwardly, each of them waiting for a parting gesture, before she said a shy goodnight, and turned to unlock the door.

Stephanie's concerns about Troy being different from her other boyfriends, and not expressing love in conventional ways, had become a deeper concern involving the need to understand the reasons for his behaviour. She had suggested to Michael that they meet at the supermarket where they'd met before. That way, they could combine their fortnightly shopping with catch-up. It wouldn't look like a secret rendezvous, and Michael might help her better understand her husband.

'I know he was abused,' she told Michael. 'He told me…said his father hit him and his mother, and that it happened more than once.'

'Yes,' Michael answered. 'He had a tough time growing up.'

'When did it start,' Stephanie asked, 'and how long…'

'The early years at primary school, and on and off after that.' He didn't want to go into details. He didn't know them all anyway. To say more would be a betrayal.

Yet Stephanie was probing for more. 'But I gather it was pretty bad.'

Michael was a little surprised. Perhaps there were personal things Troy had shared with him and not with Stephanie. He might have thought it would shock her sensibilities. 'It was bad,' was all he could say.

They were quiet for a minute.

'His mother…what a lovely woman…the thought of her being knocked around, and he's so protective of her. I'm worried about him, Michael,' she changed tack. 'I went to the internet. It said abuse in childhood increased the likelihood of problems like depression, alcoholism, multiple personality disorders and sexual things.'

'And has it, do you think?' he asked tentatively.

'Drinking's not a problem. He has mood swings…he's certainly depressed. And abused children are supposed to have more health problems later…headaches, arthritis, stroke, heart disease, that sort of thing…even obesity.'

'I agree the abuse has soured his outlook on life…a little anyway,' he added quickly when he saw her frown, 'but as for the rest, all those medical things, that's jumping the gun, isn't it?'

'Of course it is,' she answered, brightening. 'And how's everything with you, Michael?'

'Up and down, but pretty much the same.' He didn't want to share what happened three Saturday nights ago. He might tell her one day. But it was still too raw.

They left together, grateful to have seen each other.

Outside Woolworths on the way to the car park, an infant boy of three or four was sitting at the entrance of the shop refusing to move, his face puckered with defiance. His young mother was trying to pull him to his feet, pleading with him.

'No,' he shouted, 'no!'

His mother's pleas became imperative. 'You get up now, Matthew.' But Matthew wouldn't. 'If you're not on your feet after five…' and she began counting, 'one, two, three…'

'Four, six, seben,' the boy mocked.

People walked past pretending not to notice. It was no business of theirs.

The mother, furious, hauled the boy to his feet, lifting him by the arm, and hit his bare legs with several hard smacks. The boy screamed and started bawling. The mother stood still, stricken. Tears coursed down her face. Passers-by were curious now. Some were looking hostile. A security guard approached to investigate.

Michael and Stephanie had come to a stop. Michael watched fascinated, desperately sorry for the woman. He could see her pain revisited on Stephanie's face, and watched as she hurried across to the woman and held her. The woman was grateful and hugged Stephanie, burying her face in Stephanie's neck. They stood clinging to each other for fully a minute. The boy had stopped crying and was looking at his mother and the strange woman curiously.

Michael and Troy met in Blackheath the following Sunday. Michael had met an old friend who lived there. Troy was returning from relatives in Orange and had to pass through along the Great Western Highway.

Blackheath is a well-to-do address in the upper Blue Mountains with a thriving community of restaurants, pubs, bookshops, galleries, supermarkets and antique barns.

They had hot chocolates and scones at The Banksia in the main street, and drove down Govett's Leap Road to the lookout. They read the Govett's Leap plaque, looked across the blue haze of gums to distant peaks, and felt small. It was hot and the mountain air was spiced with eucalyptus. It was a few hundred metres to Bridal Veil Falls, where sheets of water plunged, rising in spray from the rocks below.

They stood at the fence, several metres from the edge, and each thought of the wafer-thin line between life and death, a few steps away, steps taken accidentally or in despair.

Troy was the first to comment. 'It'd be so easy, wouldn't it?' he said.

'You're not thinking about it?'

'Why would you think that?'

'Apparently, it's not that uncommon…people in a high place wanting to jump.'

'No.' Troy's reply was unemphatic.

They watched the falls for several minutes.

'You seem to have been a bit down lately,' Michael said, thinking that enough time had passed since their talk about jumping. 'Is everything all right?'

'Have you been talking to Stephanie?'

Michael had to admit he had been, but Troy didn't seem to mind.

'What did she say?' There was an edge to his voice.

'Only that you seemed to be depressed.' Michael had no need to be evasive. 'And she's worried about you, wants to understand, help if she can.'

'I suppose I am, depressed that is, but I'm always that way. It's me. I sometimes wonder if it's who I am, or whether something's made me that way…blocked out the real me.'

'I think you know the answer to that.'

'Yeah, I do. Mum's been able to move on. I haven't.'

'If your mum can, you can.'

'Sounds simple, doesn't it? Do you really believe I can change what I am?'

'I'd like to think so. Perhaps we can all change if we know what we want…what we want to change into.' Michael hoped his answer didn't sound like that of the self-help guru who had once infuriated Troy.

'Do you really think people know? Can you honestly say what you want, I mean really want, in the long term?'

'I know one thing for certain. I want to live for someone else, and I want to live in them.'

'You mean Tiffany?'

'Yes, Tiffany.'

'Don't take this the wrong way, but do you think you're a little obsessed? You've been running after her for quite a while now. What if she doesn't want you to live for her, or in her, whatever that means?'

Michael was silent, and a little ruffled. A family passed behind them. Two children were talking excitedly. The girl was doing cartwheels on the grass.

'And you, Troy, are you trying to break free from…from something that's consuming you?'

'We're back where we started. I don't want to see things the way I do. I want to think differently. I want to feel differently. No one can possibly know how much. Saying it is one thing, but doing it…'

'There must be help, professional help.'

'Do you know, Michael, there are times when I have so much anger bottled up inside me, I think I'm going to explode. Little things get to me, nothing things, and I lose my cool.'

'There are doctors trained in anger management.'

'You know what worries me the most, Michael? At times, I've come so close to hitting Stephanie. I've said cruel things to her. I've felt my hand clenching into a fist at my side. It doesn't take long to realise she's done nothing wrong, that she's trying desperately to understand, and I feel terrible. I've been so close to…'

He fell silent, and Michael had nothing else to offer. He didn't think there was anything unusual about his own family. He couldn't say there was never any anger, but the little that did come to the fore was internalised, surfacing occasionally with an ironic comment or hasty riposte.

'This is good,' Troy said almost in a whisper. 'Yes, this is doing me good, being with you, looking at that,' and he waved a hand in a broad gesture at the valley and distant hills of gums, turning charcoal in the fading light of dusk, a spell of halted time, and at a sunset of hot pink and apricot.

'Look at us, Michael,' he was more cheerful, 'two innocent little schoolboys, and look at us now.'

Rosenman was the name of the psychologist, or was he a psychiatrist? Troy wasn't sure. He was a slight man with a high forehead, wore a bow tie, and had small eyes that peered through the thickest lenses he'd ever seen.

Troy hadn't been entirely deaf to Michael's suggestions of seeking professional help. Stephanie had also suggested it in a roundabout way. But neither Stephanie, Michael nor his own mother knew that he had come. And he had made the appointment half-heartedly, not believing it could do much good.

'I'm concerned that I get so angry,' he told Rosenman, and that I might lash out and hurt someone, I mean hurt them physically, especially someone I love.'

Not surprisingly, the doctor wanted a full account of Troy's history, particularly that relating to any abuse he had suffered. He also wanted to know if Troy had abused anyone.

'My history?' Troy stammered. 'Does that mean I'm going to abuse my family?' he asked when the doctor had listened patiently to his story, jotting down the odd note. 'When I have a family, that is.'

'The majority of people who abuse others were abused as children.' Rosenman was clear and straightforward. Troy liked that. 'But the reverse is not true. In other words, most people who are abused as children do not end up abusing others.'

Troy was making sense of Rosenman's explanation when the doctor, clearly sensitive to Troy's burden, continued. 'Just because you have a history of being abused as a child, Mr Douglas, doesn't mean that you are on the path of continuing with the cycle of abuse.'

Troy felt some relief. 'So what do you suggest I do, doctor?'

'You've done the most important thing already,' Rosenman answered. 'The fact that you are worried about abusing others, and being aware about that potential abuse, means that you are being honest with yourself. That is the critical starting point.'

Rosenman leant back in his chair to explain. 'There's cognitive behavioural therapy, and other therapies that target your anger patterns and your distorted opinions. They offer modelling and reflection.'

But Troy wasn't listening. Hadn't Rosenman said that it was a good start acknowledging the problem, being honest with yourself? He convinced himself that he had been confirmed in his own prognosis. He would leave the office feeling virtuous. He had met the problem head-on. Or was he the shipwrecked passenger grabbing at a piece of flotsam in a mountainous sea?

Stephanie called a fortnight later, asking Michael for a meeting. It was a Monday and she didn't want to wait till their usual Thursday time. She was immaculately dressed in a white wrap-around skirt and an emerald-coloured blouse, an attempt, or so Michael thought, to offset the strain etched on her sallow face.

She quickly hugged and kissed him on the cheek, and sat down. Her hands were trembling. Her jaw was clenched. Michael was immediately alerted. There was something resolute, something business-like about her manner.

'I'm leaving him,' she said, not looking at him, and fidgeting by rearranging the cutlery on the tablecloth.

Michael looked at her in disbelief. 'Why?'

'He hit me, Michael. Can you believe that? He hit me! You'd think he'd be the very last person…'

Michael struggled for the right question. If he asked whether it was just the once, she might feel he was dismissing it as not too serious. 'Tell me what happened,' he said, knowing he'd hear the whole story. He did.

'From the very beginning, he was moody, and as time went on the mood swings became greater. Remember my telling you that? He could be wonderful, gentle and kind, but he could change suddenly.'

She stopped to have a sip of her coffee. Her hand still trembled. Michael could see the pain in her face.

'He had to give a presentation on the environment a week or so ago to Rotary. It was important to him, I get that, and he asked me if I would mind having his suit dry-cleaned. It had been sitting creased in the cupboard with a few dirty marks, and it smelled. I forgot. Well, from the reaction, you'd think I'd done it on purpose.'

She was becoming increasingly emotional. Her words were a haemorrhage. 'He screamed at me and was hostile for hours. He changed after his talk was a great success, and apologised. More than apologised – he was so contrite, said he'd do anything to make it up to me.'

'And he hit you,' Michael prompted when she'd been silent for a while.

'No, not then,' she answered. 'That happened on Friday night. I came home with a big dent in the side of the car. He yelled again and slapped me across the face.'

Michael could see that there was more make-up on one side of her face.

'What's more,' she added, close to tears, 'it wasn't my fault. Someone ran into my car in the car park when I was shopping, and they left without leaving any contact details.'

They sat in silence finishing their coffee.

'You don't think it's a bit premature?' He asked tentatively. 'I mean leaving him. That's so final.'

'I don't think I ever told you, Michael,' she said, having regained her composure. 'I used to spend some of my Christmas holidays with my Auntie Sheila. We were very fond of each other…still are. My uncle Bob seemed a lovely bloke, but he began to mistreat her. At first, it was getting angry and verbally abusing her, but it escalated until he knocked out her two front teeth and blinded her in one eye. I remember her saying her greatest regret was not getting out when it first began.' There were tears in her eyes as she told the story.

'But do you think what Troy has done…'

'Michael,' she interrupted stonily, 'I have no intention of waiting around to find out. Ever since what happened to Auntie Sheila…'

'What was Troy's reaction?' Michael didn't need to ask.

'That was the hard part.' Stephanie was distressed again. 'He was shattered. Kept saying it was history repeating itself, how sorry he was, how it would never happen again, how he'd been to a psychologist to get advice…did you know about that?'

'No.'

'Michael, I don't hate him. There's still a lot of love there.' She reached into her bag for a tissue. 'But I'm not prepared to live like that. Can you do me a favour?'

'Anything, Steph.'

'He more than ever needs your support now.'

Troy answered the door to Michael the same day. His eyes looked black and sunken like craters in a Greek mask. He was unshaven. His place was a mess. He closed the door quickly behind them, and began talking before they'd both sat down.

'I know why you're here. It's hard to explain,' he said. 'I was so angry, but as soon as I heard the sound of the slap – it wasn't a dull thud, more like the crack of a pistol shot – I realised what I'd done, but it was too late to take it back.'

Troy was staring ahead. His eyes were dead, pain without feeling. 'I'll never forget Steph standing there, still as a rock, her eyes wide in disbelief, watching her face reassemble into…into I don't know what, a simulacrum. And I was in as much shock as she was. I couldn't move. I should have. God, I regret that. I should have rushed to her, tried to hold her, pleaded forgiveness.'

'Is it too late, Troy?' Michael asked uncertainly. He remembered his talk with Stephanie, and her unwavering conviction that all was lost. She'd always been a strong woman, but…

'She's gone, you know,' he answered. 'She was crying when she said goodbye, gave me a kiss, wished me well. It nearly tore me apart. I was standing upstairs at the window as she went out the gate with her suitcase. I watched from behind the curtain as she struggled to put it in the boot. I could have helped her. Never, ever, have I felt so empty. My whole life was falling apart. She didn't look up at the window…why didn't she look up and wave…why?'

Michael shrugged. 'She was too angry, Troy. Perhaps if you wait a few days and let things settle…convince her that you'll get all the professional help on offer. Stephanie's very understanding. If she knows you're really serious, she might even go with you.'

Troy continued with his own thoughts. 'You know she even took Barnie. He's the fluffy toy bear she's had since kindergarten. Barnie sits on the bed. The last thing we do at the end of each day is to say goodnight to Barnie. She's coming back for more of her stuff in a day or two, and said she wants me out within a week.'

'Well, that's the perfect chance for the two of you to talk.' Michael tried to sound upbeat.

Troy shook his head, still staring ahead. His voice had quietened to a whisper. 'I think she's a lot better off without me.'

7

It was the second time Margaret Thurgood had called him wanting him to visit. He was a little alarmed, because she had returned home, and had come back to be with Tiffany. While potential mothers-in-law are often the subject of light-hearted satire, Michael enjoyed her company, and wished her daughter could be as easy to get along with.

She kissed him on the cheek and led him to the lounge where they'd sat before. Since she began visiting Tiffany, Margaret had made changes to the unit. The room was drenched in sunlight from open windows that had always been closed. There were several photographs in gilt frames, and fresh flowers on the buffet and coffee table.

'She's gone away for a while, Michael,' Margaret said, and reached for his hand.

Michael was well aware of her percipience. She knew what Tiffany meant to him, even if Tiffany had not spoken to her.

'Gone where?' he asked, feeling he'd been punched in the chest.

'Believe it or not, Michael, I don't know.' She looked serious. 'Tiffany thought it better I didn't know.'

Michael believed her. He would probably have known if she were hiding something. 'Why?' he asked, suddenly feeling threatened.

'I think you know all about Paul by now,' she answered, and waited for his reply.

'I know he meant a lot to her,' he replied, 'but she hasn't told me much. I don't know the details.'

'Well, since he killed himself...'

'Killed himself?'

'Since he died at terribly high speed in the car crash, Tiffany has never been the same. They fought like cats and dogs, but they were very close.'

She paused and Michael didn't speak, sensing that this was all leading somewhere.

'She was devastated at the time, and now just moons around. Well, you know what she's like.'

'Margaret,' he was becoming impatient, 'she's gone away because…'

'Because she's finding it hard to deal with, I suppose.'

'How long's she going to be away?'

'She wouldn't say. But I gather it's more than a few days.'

They were silent for half a minute, before Margaret could sense what was on his mind.

'You're thinking she's gone away because of you,' she said, squeezing his hand. 'There could be some truth in that. I know she cares for you, Michael, but it's probably another pressure, another claim on her that she wants to run away from.'

'I suppose there's nothing I can do, then,' he said. He was feeling fragile.

'I think it's important, Michael,' and he realised this was the main purpose of the meeting, 'that you give her space. That's the kindest thing you can do for her now. And it might be the best thing for you too in the long run.' To soften the confronting tone of their talk, she brought out her scones, made coffee, and asked him about his work.

It took several days for Michael to decide whether to be guided by Margaret's request. He finally decided that it would do no harm to find out where she was. That way, he could decide later whether to see her or not. There was some security in knowing.

With this impasse out of the way, his first step was to see if there were any clues in her unit as to her whereabouts. Margaret had returned home again the morning after their last meeting. He'd known for some weeks now where she kept her spare key, and let himself in.

It was empty and eerily bare, neat, everything in its place, but lacking the soul it had possessed a few days earlier. Or was it just that the owner was needed to invest it with 'soul'? He looked around the living room, but didn't find anything helpful. That was not surprising because he didn't even know what he was looking for. She didn't want to be found.

He went to the bedroom, sat on the bed, and bounced on it like a child. He noticed the picture of Paul, now given pride of place on her bedside table. 'Do you know what you've done?' he said to it.

What did I expect, he told himself when he left, secreting the key in its hiding-place. But his spirits were dampened.

He went to their usual Thursday-night restaurant, hoping that she might have second thoughts about staying away, and be there to meet him. The restaurant, like her unit, didn't seem special any more. He'd never noticed before how tired the décor was.

'Drinks for you and the lady?' the waiter asked. 'The usual?'

'Mine, yes, thank you,' he said pleasantly. 'Not sure about the lady yet.'

She didn't come, and he ate his meal in silence. The waiters watched sympathetically. More often than not, they agreed, it was the woman who waited in vain.

An attractive brunette sat at the bar sipping a cocktail, bare legs crossed in a black working skirt. She looked in his direction more than once, trying to catch his eye. He noticed. She was interested. But he didn't return her interest. That wasn't a solution. He left depressed.

After his school day, he'd walk the streets, hoping he might see her in some of their familiar haunts. He'd even go to the supermarket at night, and not to shop. On the third day, he saw her. It was nearing five o'clock.

She was a block away, walking in the same direction as him. She wore her black slacks, and a lemon top he hadn't seen before. Her blonde hair was combed to her shoulders and bobbed as she walked.

'Tiffany,' he heard the word escape his lips, and he hurried after her.

She was hurrying too, and he had to run to get closer. She crossed at traffic lights, and he didn't get to the crossing in time. He waited, begging the green walk sign to flash. He was tempted to call out, but he would have had to scream to be heard, and there were people on both sides of the street waiting to cross. Whatever would they think?

Green at last, and he'd seen her enter a shop, a grocery shop. He hurried across the street, and waited a few doors away, pretending to examine something in a shop window. Following her inside wasn't an option. He didn't want a scene.

She was only inside for a few minutes, and turned abruptly once she was outside to walk away from him again, carrying a bag of shopping.

He followed. The streets were crowded with workers heading home, and he thought it might be helpful to see where she went rather than stop her on the footpath. It would be easier to talk in the peace of wherever she was staying.

The crowd was thinning, and she was making her way towards a bus stop. He had to act now or risk losing her.

He ran up to her. 'Tiff,' he called, placing a hand on her shoulder. 'It's me.'

She turned. It wasn't her! She looked at him in fright, and then in suspicion, before her face relaxed.

'Oh. I'm terribly sorry.' His heart sank. 'I didn't mean, I really didn't mean…'

'I know you didn't.' She was kind. She rescued him. 'I hope you find this Tiff,' she said, gave his arm a consoling pat, and turned for the bus that had just arrived.

She'd been gone a week when he received a letter. He recognised her writing on the envelope, and tore it open.

Dear Michael,

I had to get away. I'm sorry I didn't tell you first, but I know you wouldn't have liked me going and would have tried to stop me. I hope you understand.

I'm all right. Just need some thinking time, and space. I'm quite comfortable so there's no need to worry about me. Please don't try to find me.

Tiffany.

Michael was hurt and angry. It was hardly a keepsake. Not a letter you pressed with a rose between the pages of a book to look at with nostalgia on some distant rainy day. He paced his room, brandishing the letter and talking aloud. Where was the 'and how are you, Michael?' Did she give a damn? Where was the 'I'm missing you so much.' And what of her signing off? 'Tiffany.' Not 'love Tiffany', or 'thinking of you', not even 'fond regards'. There was no feeling, no affection. And there was no mention of how long she was going to stay away.

He rolled the letter into a ball and threw it furiously against the wall. It dropped onto the carpet, and he kicked at it, missing and nearly losing his balance.

He brooded for a few days before he thought of another plan of attack. Deirdre. Why on earth had he not thought of Deirdre before? They were the best of friends. If anyone knew where she was, Deirdre would.

He didn't know where she lived, but for once, or so he told himself, luck smiled upon him. He found her at the art gallery, hoping to have a third of her pictures accepted.

She recognised him and hurried across to give him a theatrical kiss, then took his arm and led him to a chaise longue.

'I need your help, Deirdre,' he said.

'For you, anything.' She still had her arm linked in his and was pressing against him as they sat down. She was over-perfumed. On his previous visit, he had tabbed Deirdre as an outrageous flirt.

'Do you know where Tiffany is?'

Deirdre said she hadn't seen Tiffany since they last met together in the gallery. She had no idea that Tiffany had gone away, and no, she had no idea where she might be. Michael thanked her, was led to her new painting which he praised generously, and made for the door.

'Michael,' she called after him, 'it's probably nothing, but when we were teenagers, Tiffany used to talk about staying at a place in Scarborough on the south coast, a beach house. But that was years ago.'

It was the best lead he'd had. It was the only lead he'd had. He thanked Deirdre, suffered another stale theatrical kiss on the lips, and left.

He drove to Scarborough the next day, admiring the lush greenery and glittering beaches of the south coast. It had been years since he'd been there but he remembered it as a small place with a pub and general store, and houses basking chalkily on the hillside.

Believing the general store to be the font of all local wisdom, he entered, stepping over a St Bernard sleeping in the doorway, and enquired there, giving a detailed description and realising, with regret, that he didn't have a single picture of Tiffany. He should have fetched the one with Paul.

'Can't say I do,' the proprietress shook her head.

'Yes, you do,' her husband said, coming out from behind the counter. 'She was in here day before yesterday. 'The pretty blonde, nice figure.'

'Trust you to notice,' the wife retorted, and they all laughed.

Michael drove around the streets of Scarborough looking for her car but didn't find it. Thinking it might have been garaged, he decided that all he could do was to park somewhere in sight of the general store and wait for her to shop. Fortunately, the store only opened from nine to five, so there was relief at night from his surveillance. He booked a room at the pub.

The first day of watching was an eternity. He sat in the car for eight hours. It was stinking hot and he kept changing position, sticking to the seat, finding it hard to get comfortable. He hurried out a few times for drinks, a sandwich and toilet breaks, scurrying back so he wouldn't miss her. He slept restlessly that night on a lumpy bed that rolled him into its middle.

At mid-afternoon on the second day, he saw her. There was no doubt this time. She parked at the other end of the street, entered the store and came our several minutes later with a heavy bag. She stopped outside the door, and for half a minute looked carefully up and down the street and across the road.

'Damn,' Michael muttered. Of course the store owners would have told her that a man was looking for her, and they would have described the man. It hadn't occurred to him. Now what was he to do? She'd be watching for his car following her.

But why the secrecy? He'd found her. Why not just walk straight up to her and tell her he'd been searching for her? Why? Because her letter had said 'please don't try to find me'. What would seeing her accomplish? She'd be angry. She didn't want to be found. Was he kidding himself that she would fall into his arms. The weight of history was against him.

For the first time, he was considering the futility of his search. Finding her had been all-consuming. He wasn't even sure what he would say to her. Margaret was right. She needed her space. A meeting would be seen as unwelcome confrontation.

She'd already driven away. He hadn't followed. He turned his car to face the beach and sat looking at the sea. He didn't know how long he stayed there, but the sun had dropped low to the horizon out at sea, a big orange ball, and the bottom of the sky was aflame. It soon darkened, but not before a rainbow arched in the sky, and a few drops of rain dotted the windscreen.

Minutes later, it was black, and he switched on the ignition. Time to go.

Michael had another dream. He was holding a sword. It was the same one his pursuer had held in his earlier dream. It had a long shiny blade that kept catching the sun. There was a foreboding about those glints on the sword. He was chasing two people, intent on doing them harm.

They were a long way away, but he was faster than they were, and was gaining on them. They knew he was following them, but didn't seem to be running as fast as they could. Perhaps they were just pacing themselves. They were jogging rather than running for their lives. As he neared, he could see that one was a man, and the other a woman. They could see the sword. He must surely have looked menacing, but it didn't seem to bother them.

They ran through the streets of the town. He was waving the sword about, but it didn't seem to bother the passers-by. Several stopped and pointed. They were laughing at him. Mothers with young children, businessmen in suits, teenage schoolgirls, old men, shop owners standing in their doorways, all laughing.

As he got closer to the man and woman, they stopped, turned to look at him, and they also laughed. They said something to each other that made them laugh more. It must have been some joke at his expense. Then they turned and hurried away.

He followed them across the street. They ran across when there was no traffic. He had to dodge several honking cars and was nearly hit. One driver shouted a few choice words. He was gaining on them with every second. They were almost in striking distance. Soon. It would be soon. They ran into a gallery, past the curator. 'It shows humankind's reaction to a complex technological world,' he said without looking up.

The man and woman exited from a side door, laughing and goading him. He gave chase but while he was close, he wasn't gaining on them any more.

They ran into a restaurant. It looked familiar. 'Your usual table, sir, madam, and you sir,' the proprietor said, looking surprised at the extra arrival. His father hailed him from the bar. 'If you need to know anything, just ask,' he said, and scuttled away.

He chased them onto a beach. The woman had slipped off her shoes on the sand, and ran, hand in hand with the man, skipping ankle-deep in the water, enjoying herself. She didn't seem to be fearful. He remained the same distance behind them, neither gaining nor retreating. He could see the imprints her tiny feet made in the drier sand, the big toe of her right foot. Sometimes they'd look around at him, and even when he raised the sword as if he were taunting them with a mock swipe, they'd laugh.

He was angry and frustrated. He'd narrowed the distance between them by so much when the chase began, but he wasn't making any ground now. He could feel a tightening in his chest.

They were running through the streets again. The buildings looked familiar. He knew he'd been there before.

The man and woman turned suddenly, and ran into an alley. They must have thought that they were eluding him. But how could they think that when he was so close behind. He remembered that alley. He'd been there before. There could be no escape for them now. It was an alley with a dead end. They'd soon discover that. He gripped the sword tightly in anticipation.

It was dark there when he entered in pursuit. Tall buildings on either side blocked out the sun. As his eyes adjusted, he could make out the woman jogging to the end of the alley, but she was alone. Where was the man? He'd disappeared. There was nowhere to go, and nowhere to hide. The only way out was to come past him, and the alley was so narrow he couldn't miss seeing him.

The woman had stopped, and watched him approach. He brandished the sword, but she wasn't scared. She gave a sweet chuckle and smiled at him.

He stood before her and raised the sword above his head in both hands, preparing to strike. There was a deafening crashing sound, louder than thunder, and the world began to spin.

Another ten days. People demonstrated on climate change in every capital city in Australia. A lone gunman shot seven students dead in a Texas school and turned the gun on himself. Petrol prices reached unheard of heights. A surprising Royal rift was foreshadowed. A tsunami destroyed a whole town in Indonesia. A priest of high status was convicted of sexual abuse.

Margaret Thurgood called. 'She's back, Michael. I got the call this morning.'

She didn't call me, he nearly said, feeling miserable, and waited.

Margaret seemed to read his silence. 'She'd only just arrived. I'm sure she'll be in touch as soon as she gets settled.'

Michael didn't know where to begin, or whether to begin at all. 'Is she all right?' was all he could say.

'I think it's better that she talk for herself, Michael,' she answered, 'but Michael…'

Her pause was portentous. Michael waited impatiently.

'It might not seem so to you, but I think she really needs you.'

He was taken by surprise. This message was different from that of their earlier talk when he'd been warned that Tiffany needed her space.

'That's hard to believe, Margaret,' he said, but not harshly. 'People who need another person usually don't disappear for three weeks without saying a word.'

'It may be hard to believe, Michael,' she was quick to answer, 'but she may not even know it herself.'

He heard nothing from her that day. She called the following morning saying she'd be free that afternoon. There was nothing particularly warm about her greeting. She even seemed to be in a hurry to get off the phone, though phone calls for Tiffany had always been for blunt messages, not for exchange of sentiment.

'I missed you,' he'd said.

'I missed you too,' she'd answered quickly, routinely.

He was anxious to see her, but there was also a certain dread. He knew the morning's wait would be difficult, so he arranged to meet Stephanie. He needed to talk, and she was a good listener. He told her everything, even the events of that harrowing Saturday night.

She was understanding. 'Let me know what happens,' she said when he was leaving, and she held him close for fully a minute.

He could feel her warmth, the softness of her body, smell the fragrance of her perfume.

A person's experiences change perceptions even of the real, the tangible. Seeing Tiffany's unit felt different. It hadn't changed, so he knew it must be him.

He waited for half a minute at the door. That shouldn't have concerned him but it did. It said something about the urgency of her need. If the door had been opened instantly, if she'd been standing there before he knocked… He knew he was being ridiculous.

'Good to see you, Michael,' she greeted him, but there was no light in her eyes. She leant forward, bending at the waist, and kissed him on the cheek at arm's length, hands-free, then walked to sit at her usual place on the lounge. Her feet were bare and she was wearing a magenta beach shift.

It was a few seconds before Michael moved. 'Shall I…' and he pointed to the kitchen.

'That'd be nice,' she answered. 'There are biscuits in the cupboard.'

He had started to make the coffee when she got up and came into the kitchen.

'I can tell you're disappointed,' she said. 'I'm sorry,' and she threw both arms around him as he turned, kettle in hand, pressing her body against his for a moment and averting her face. She gripped him fiercely before she let go. 'Now let's have that coffee.'

'Tell me about your time away,' he asked dully, after they'd been drinking in silence for a minute.

'Not much to tell,' she answered. 'I needed time out.' She didn't say why. 'I used to stay there years ago. It's nice there, unspoiled, clean air, the beach to walk along in the cool of the evening… The people in the store said a man was asking after me, or someone like me, and I thought it might have been you, but their descriptions didn't match.'

'What if it had been me?' He asked, relieved.

'I wouldn't have been too impressed,' she answered. 'I said not to search for me.'

'But your time away,' he persisted, 'has it changed how you think, how you feel?'

She was suddenly tense. 'Changed how?' She could sense what he wanted to know. 'Look, Michael, this is no romance novel,' she said, and instantly regretted it.

Michael was hurt as if he'd been felled by a sudden blow. He looked ahead, then turned to stare at her, at a gentle face, a face that now had a fragility, but a face that was a mask. He felt the feeling flowing from him like blood from a severed artery. Was it the months of unrequited affection, was it her leaving for weeks without a word, was it her final insult – this is no romance novel? It never had been.

Stephanie had embraced him warmly with concern and affection. It had felt so natural, so right, the way feeling between a man and a woman should be expressed. They weren't lovers. They were close friends. Tiffany had grabbed at him with a reluctant sense of duty. There was something aggressive about it. It had been a clash of bodies, lumpy and sinewy.

Tiffany had turned away, not wanting to meet his look.

Was this an epiphany? His decision might have been dramatic, but it had crept up slowly, surprising him.

He stood, determined, never more certain of himself. Everything had become clear.

She followed suit, alarmed, sensing the change in him.

'Goodbye, Tiffany.' His voice was loud and hard.

'Michael, I don't want…I think I need…I'd rather…' She was close to tears.

He'd later think of her distress at that moment. Was it just because she'd lost a disciple? Had she been giving all the love she had to give, however little and depleted. But it was too late.

He held her gently by the shoulders, and lightly kissed her trembling lips.

8

Resolution doesn't always spell the end of doubt. Michael was confident he'd made the right decision. He was confident he'd made the only decision. But that didn't stop him missing her. For weeks, he would live with the ambivalence. He was attracted. He was repelled. He wondered if love was ever felt as much as loss.

At times, he became angry, thinking of how shabbily he'd been treated, but he'd recall how he had been irresistibly drawn to her, and how she had been living in the shadow of another's death. He made allowances. He'd even start to ponder if he'd been sufficiently understanding. Was it her fault if she'd never felt as he had?

He kept replaying their final moments together in his mind, his standing, braced with conviction to say a final goodbye, her standing, sensing and fearing a powerful change afoot, and what he heard as stammered protests. Was he mistaken? Had he ever heard any sign of need from her before?

It was these final words that surprised him. Was it a spark in the long-sodden tinder? Had Margaret been right about Tiffany needing him, and about it not being apparent, even to her, until his support was withdrawn? Margaret had almost certainly been implying that everything in Tiffany's behaviour towards him seemed to contradict such a need.

On the first Thursday after his goodbye, he dressed to go to the restaurant. He reckoned she might turn up there hoping to see him. No, he thought, and changed his good clothes. Yes, it won't do any harm, he considered, and dressed in them again. The negative won. To do anything else would be the stuff of romance novels! He quickly put on his exercise gear, and went for a run.

He was startled and secretly pleased by her first call a few days later.

It was about how much she was missing his near-blind devotion, though she wasn't prepared to say so:

'I'm sorry, I can't hear you. Can you speak up?'

'It's Tiffany, Michael.'

'Tiffany…how are you?'

'All right, and you?'

'Oh, you know, trying to keep busy.'

'Why trying? Is there something stopping you?'

'Thinking about lots of things.'

'Am I one of them, Michael?'

'Yes.'

'Are you missing me, then?'

'I miss the good times we shared.'

'I wasn't sure about meeting on Thursday night.'

'Did you go?'

'I wasn't asked.'

'Did you want me to ask? Surely you didn't expect me to, not after…'

Long silence.

'Well, I suppose I'd better go, then. Is there anything you want to…'

Her second call, a week later, was about her need of him, but stopped short of owning strong feelings for him. The only strong feelings were about herself, and she became more and more tearful.

'Michael, you said in your last call you were missing me.'

'Missing the good times we had.'

'Whatever. Well, I've missed them too. And there were a lot of them. Do you want to have more of those times, Michael?'

'Tiffany, I made a decision, and I didn't make it lightly.'

'Don't you regret it, Michael, just a little?'

'It's hard, Tiff, I'll admit that…'

'Michael, please, I want to see you again. I need to see you again.'

'But why, Tiffany?'

'What do you want me to say, Michael? You always do this to me. Always analysing. Why do two people want to see each other?'

'Sometimes it's because their feeling for each other is…is…'

Silence.

If there'd been uncertainty in Michael's mind about the finality of his decision, there was none after this second call.

A fortnight later, he heard from Margaret again. A text on his mobile asked him to visit and suggested a time. She'd returned to Sydney yet again.

It was a different Margaret Thurgood, anxious and drawn. He'd never noticed the lines etched on her face before, the farinaceous complexion. The polish and composure had gone, and he missed the banter that went on between them.

'She's not well at all, Michael. She's not eating or sleeping.' Margaret was leaning heavily against him, not apparently aware of doing so. 'She's wasting away, looks like a ghost. I'm going over there tomorrow to stay. I thought you might want to know. I thought you should know.' She sipped her coffee with a trembling hand.

'Has a doctor…' Michael began.

'She refuses to go. It's up to me now.'

'Where is she now?'

'She's gone to see Deirdre. Says Deirdre's good for her.'

'I'm so sorry, Margaret,' Michael mumbled, not sure if she were pointing an accusing finger at him.

'That Paul,' she said stonily. To Michael's relief, she was pointing the finger in another direction. 'He was a real tearaway. I never thought he was right for Tiffany.'

Michael wondered what a tearaway was, but thought better of asking. He got the gist of it.

'Now, if she'd met you first…' Normally she would have smiled or nudged him. There would have been teasing between them. But there was no light-heartedness now.

'Margaret,' Michael was feeling more relaxed, 'you don't think I played a part in this, do you? Could I have done anything…'

'No, Michael.' Her answer was firm. 'You were the only stable thing she had.'

Michael nodded with relief.

'In these last weeks, I kept wondering whether I could enlist your help. If I thought it might make a difference to Tiffany, I wouldn't have hesitated. But how does anyone know? What would you do anyway? Why plead with you to make a sacrifice of yourself, when that's all it would probably end up being.'

Stephanie was anxious to know what happened between Michael and Tiffany, and she also wanted to talk to him about her meeting with Troy. Michael knew him better than anyone, perhaps even more than she did.

She had returned to their unit, while Troy, against his wishes, had little option but to go. His guilt over hitting her had robbed him of any moral high ground.

So they met at her place, a top-floor two-bedroom unit that was attractively furnished with a carefully considered balance of the old and new. It somehow breathed with Stephanie's personality, an aura missing in Tiffany's place.

'You've made it really nice,' he told her, recalling it from his earlier days with her, and doing a quick walk around.

'Yes, we made a few changes, but Troy left it up to me. But enough of my place. I want to hear about you and Tiffany. But coffee first, and iced vovos. I remembered how you used to love them. Just leave a couple for me.' She laughed.

He told her everything that had happened with Tiffany at their last meeting. He told her about Tiffany's rough obligatory hug, the accusing look on her face when she'd said their relationship was no romance novel. He told her how she'd trembled with his final goodbye kiss. And he told her about the two recent phone calls, trying to remember the exact words, calls that were about her need. He even mentioned the small part that she had played in holding him.

She listened, watching him closely, seeing the clouds cross and re-cross his eyes, hearing the faltering in his voice.

When he'd finished, he'd asked her if his reactions were unreasonable or whether they were just the straws that broke the camel's back. She had been surprised that he'd continued for so long with the relationship in the face of such indifference, but she didn't say so. She did say that he'd been more than reasonable, and he took heart, knowing that she was someone who always said what she thought.

'I know, Steph, with no doubt at all, if I go back, nothing will change. It'll be just the same. It's so sad,' he said, 'when it comes to an end like that, when two reasonable people attempt to speak to each other, and it's just another dose of poison.'

Stephanie didn't answer. She reached for his hand and they sat in silence.

'Your turn,' Michael eventually said. He didn't have to ask if she wanted to talk about Troy. It was the main purpose of his visit.

'He rang, begging to see me. We met at Brooklyn, where we'd sometimes go for a morning tea or lunch. I thought it'd be safer outside than in. Oh, Michael,' her eyes were already watery, 'he was dressed…well, he was way overdressed for Brooklyn, trousers with a sharp crease, his best shirt, clean-shaven, new haircut. He so wanted to impress.'

Michael had a clear picture of him, and his heart went out to his friend. He could relate to that.

'He was like the little school boy, painfully shy, offering a girl a sweetie. Can you believe it, Michael, he'd bought flowers, all wrapped in green cellophane. He'd never given me flowers before. It wasn't hard to tell what was coming, something rehearsed, I reckoned. We had coffee at the café, and spoke about friends we have in common. We spoke about the fires up north and the floods overseas. It was so false. I could tell he was fit to burst with impatience. He started when we'd left the kiosk and found a seat in the park, you remember, up on the hill looking over the water where we used to go.'

'I know the very seat,' Michael answered. 'Fond memories, Steph.'

'Well, he started telling me things I hadn't heard before. I knew he and his mother had been hit, but I didn't know the awful detail…how once he tried to defend his mother, who'd been slapped across the face, and how his father punched him in the face and came after him with his heavy studded belt, how he hid in the wardrobe for hours.'

'Yes, he told me that the day after it happened,' Michael replied. 'He was traumatised. It has stayed with him all these years.'

'He told me of other incidents.' Stephanie was crying, and Michael put his arm around her shoulders.

'He went on and on, Michael. I'm not crying because I'm still upset hearing about all the abuse. That was certainly terrible. I'm crying because I'm still annoyed. I didn't need to hear it all. Not then. He could have said it all before. He was trying to make me feel sorry. I felt he was trying to soften me up, as if it was some sort of tactic to get my forgiveness, to lure me back. I had to stop him. I interrupted. "Troy," I said, "I know you've been abused. I know you've had a childhood you wouldn't wish on your worst enemy. I can feel your pain. But that's not the real issue here." He was upset. He was quiet for a while, and he said, "Yes, I know." That's when he started to beg, pleading with me to take him back, telling me that he loved me and it would never happen again. "Please give me another chance, Steph," and "I promise I won't let you down." "But Troy, I said, you might only have hit me once, but I've seen you clench your fists, you've screamed at me a number of times, and been in a foul temper most of the time. And we've only been married a matter of months. How can you be so sure you won't hit me again…or even worse?"'

'And weren't you tempted to go back with him?' Michael asked. 'Don't you think he was contrite, that he meant what he said?'

'I have no doubt he meant it, Michael. Most people have good intentions. The world is full of well-intentioned people, but how often are they followed through?'

Michael had no answer, and while Stephanie's decision seemed harsh, he could see the wisdom in it.

'I'm also upset,' she continued, 'and I know it might seem unfair, with how Troy is behaving now. The begging, the grovelling, it seems so… There's no dignity, it's unmanly. That sounds terrible, but I'm losing respect for him. At Brooklyn, he seemed almost pathetic. Michael, I know you think I'm acting prematurely, but I can't, I just can't take the risk of going back. And I don't feel the same about him any more.'

Michael wasn't prepared to argue. He still had his arm around her shoulders. She was leaning against him. He was intrigued by her saying that she didn't feel the same any more, and wanted to ask if she thought she'd made a mistake with Troy in the first place. But he dared not. So he allowed her to continue.

'I remember you telling me years ago that someone said whoever deals with monsters should make sure in the process they don't also become a monster.'

'Nietzsche.'

'Yes, Nietzsche.' She stood up and stretched, smoothing her skirt. 'I'll get more coffee. She seemed relieved, like someone who had cleared the air. 'Wise words, Mr Nietzsche.'

Michael had trouble finding him. Where had he gone? He went to the supermarket several times, and even walked around the streets in the futile hope of seeing him. The proverbial place for men to go when their lives were falling apart is the pub. But Troy didn't drink.

He remembered Troy's fondness for snooker. He'd been a good player in his teenage years, and the local club had a couple of snooker tables.

'Yeah, Troy, that was his name, cleaned us up real good,' a man at one of the tables said.

'Would you know where I could find him?'

'Nah, but Graham might know. Graham,' he called to a man who was returning to the table with a tray of drinks, 'you were talking a lot to that bloke who played with us a couple of weeks ago, the really good player, called himself Troy. Did he say where he lived?'

It was a small suite of two rooms on top of a dilapidated grocery shop. A bedroom with bathroom, and a sitting room with kitchen attached. Michael had to climb steep and rickety wooden stairs on the outside of the building to get there.

Troy opened the door without surprise, and ushered him inside. There were dark rings around his eyes, he was unshaven, and in bare feet. He wore tattered shorts and a frayed and food-stained polo top. He showed no emotion at Michael's visit.

The sitting room held an impressive oak table, but the carpet and sofa were worn, and the walls were a parchment colour. Previous tenants must have been heavy smokers.

The sink in the tiny kitchen was full of unwashed plates. There were empty cardboard food boxes on the bench.

'Don't say it,' were Troy's first words.

'Don't say what?' Perhaps it was the look on his face. 'I wasn't going to say anything.'

They sat in silence for a minute. Sometimes, Michael reckoned, dialogue was overrated. He had no intention of interrogating Troy. Being together was a sufficient show of support.

'How are things?' he eventually asked. It was a tame enough opening that could be asked of anyone at any time.

'I saw my mother,' Troy started to talk in a near-whisper. 'And Adrian of course. Happy as…what's that expression? Pigs in mud.'

'That must have been a comfort.'

'They wanted me to go and live with them.'

'Why not, Troy? A little bit of tender loving care wouldn't go amiss right now.'

'I'm better off alone. I don't want to be killed with kindness. She was fussing around me. "We'll have all your favourites, lamb pie, pork casserole, and sweet and sour," she said. "Do you play golf?" Adrian asked "I can get you into the club. It'd be fun."'

'And you don't want it?'

Troy didn't answer. He continued with his own thoughts.

'I know it's hard, darling, she'd said, and she started to cry. You have to let it go. Yeah. Sure. And how do I do that, I felt like saying, but I didn't. "Hate ties us too closely to our enemies," she said.'

He paused, and Michael resisted interrupting his thoughts.

'She could let it go. Why can't I? My greatest concern, Michael,' he said, 'is that what I am, how I am, has nothing to do with what my father did to me. I've wondered if I'm making him a scapegoat. Perhaps it's just me, who I am and always have been. We had that talk once about whether people can change. No, I don't want it,' he answered Michael's earlier question as an afterthought.

More silence.

'I killed him, you know,' Troy said, looking vacantly towards the single window.

'What!' Michael, shocked, looked at him in disbelief. He seemed unmoved by the declaration.

'Don't look so surprised. I thought you knew.'

'No, I never thought…I didn't…'

'A morning lecture was cancelled so I came home early. Mum was playing her midweek tennis. My father had a flexi-day and was fixing the eaves. He came down from where he was working when he saw me arrive, and we chatted for a while, even had morning tea. He could be nice when he wasn't on the grog. Asked me about my studies, sports, that sort of thing. Even asked after you.'

Troy's words were slow and deliberate. Michael was mesmerised. This was a revelation.

'Better get back to it, he'd said after a while, and went upstairs where he had to lean half out of the window to reach the broken part of the eaves. I followed him. "Place is falling apart," he said. "If only your mother spent a little more time looking after it, and a little less…" I felt the hate and the rage building up inside me. It took over. In defining mum as the wrongdoer, the culprit, he was labelling himself as the victim, or dragon slayer. She did everything, Michael. Everything that needed doing in and around the house, she did it. She wasn't allowed to work. Bizarre, isn't it, how a person's fiction can become their truth.'

Michael was silent, more from shock than not having something to say.

'I was beside myself. He was sitting on the windowsill, half out of the window, leaning back to reach the eaves. I rushed at him and pushed. He was off-balance, so it didn't take much, and he was gone, gone, and it was all so silent, not a cry, not even the sound of escaping breath, or a thump when he hit the ground.'

Troy was still staring towards the window, unmoved by the telling of his story, indifferent to Michael's reaction. And Michael wasn't about to disturb the flow of Troy's story.

'I walked slowly to the window and looked down. You probably remember the top storey is three floors up. You'll hate me for saying this, Michael, but I hoped he was dead. If he wasn't, there'd be hell to pay for it. I saw him, lying sort of crumpled, one leg tucked under him, and his head on a rock, the sandstone edging to the garden.'

Michael watched Troy for a hint of emotion. There was none.

'Anyway, I walked down the stairs and into the garden where he was lying. I could tell he was dead. There was blood coming out his ears and mouth. His eyes were open, fixed in a stare, a sort of surprised look.'

'What did you feel at that moment?' Michael was curious.

'Nothing. No, that's not right. I did feel something. Pathos perhaps. He looked so pitiful. This man who once loved me, I do believe that, but who also terrified me, hurt me, lying there looking so…so…diminished.'

'So when did your mother come home?'

'I washed and dried up the morning tea things, went upstairs to see if there were any signs of my having been there, and raced back to uni. I knew a woman came in early that afternoon to fetch ironing, and she would ring the police. You probably remember I was with you when the call came. I hurried back. Mum was close behind. The police were already there. Of course I told them that he must have fallen after I'd left around mid-morning. It wasn't hard for anyone to believe that he'd fallen from the window. There were even scratch marks from his boots there to prove it. Mum was naturally very upset, and my silence was seen as shock. The police, the neighbours, everyone was so kind. I was given special consideration in my studies.'

After a long silence, Michael asked who else knew about it. 'Does your mum know? Does Steph know?' He thought Stephanie might have told him already if she had known. It would be hard to keep a secret like that, and she would have known she could trust him.

'Remember our pact back at school,' he said wryly. 'Only you, Michael. Only you know.'

'And how do you feel about it all now? I mean, how has it been living with it for all these years?'

Troy's answer was impersonal, even cryptic. 'We're all human. I suppose everyone's death reduces us a little.'

9

'Tommo came back from the gorge this morning. Said he saw a jumper.'

'What, this morning?'

'Yeah, here he comes. Ask him yourself.'

'Heard you saw a jumper this morning, Tommo.'

'Yes, 'bout eleven.'

'Where?'

'Just next to the falls. Climbed over the fence.'

'Well, are you gonna tell us what you saw?'

'Give us a chance. I went down to the lookout with Debbie and the kids. Such a lovely day, thought we'd have a picnic lunch. Deb's been at me for weeks. We never do nice things any more, she said. Groan, moan. All right, I said, and I went to check if the blankets were in the boot…'

'Tommo, we don't want your family history. Just tell us what you saw.'

'All right. Keep yer shirt on. Nice-looking bloke, well dressed, didn't take much notice of 'im. There were lots of tourists walking around, lots of kids. "Dad! Dad!" Ellie tugged at my shirt. "Look at that man over the—" I looked and he'd climbed over the fence and walked to the edge.'

'Go on, mate. Look, if you're upset, you don't have to…'

'No, it's all right. A few others had noticed, and had stopped to look. "Oh, my God," I heard a woman cry. Her husband called out, he called out, "Sir, are you all right, do you need to talk to someone, do you want help?" But he didn't answer, didn't even look around. He just stepped out, stepped out and disappeared.'

'What did everyone do?'

'The woman who'd seen him climb over the fence screamed, kept screaming. Most couldn't move, just stood there, stuck to the ground. One family, religious types, crossed themselves, and bowed their heads. Can you believe that? Praying for his soul, I suppose. Lost soul, I'd say.'

'Here's Brett. He'll know more. Brett, Tommo saw the jumper.'

'I've been hearing from a number of witnesses. A lot of people are really upset. It's not every day…'

'What can you tell us?'

'Troy Douglas, thirty-two, from Sydney. He made it easy for us. Wallet had credit cards, licence, phone numbers, addresses. Of course that doesn't tell us why. We'll probably never know that.'

'There's probably a mother, might be a wife and kids, all hearing about it now. I'll bet they had no idea.'

'Yeah, they often don't. Are you all right, Tommo? You're looking a bit green around the gills.'

'Poor bugger! Not you, Tommo. That Troy bloke!'

It happened only a few days after their meeting, and Michael was obviously upset at losing his best friend. He accused himself for not having read the signs when they'd spoken, and wondered if there was anything he could have done. He believed there was anxiety in everyone, that it was part of being human, but he should have seen the anxiety in Troy, or at least better interpreted the diversions that disguised it, the bravado, the routines, the jokes, or in Troy's case, the retreat from life.

He'd once asked Troy if he thought their lives were programmed, laid out before them, and Troy was strong in his denial. He would have argued strongly that it was his decision, made of his own free will.

He had to wonder about Troy's timing. Was it only their childhood pact that made Troy admit to what he'd done to his father? Troy knew his secret was safe with Michael, but perhaps the telling released some blockage in him, opened the sluice gates. He may have already planned his end, and the telling was a final gesture, a cleaning of the slate.

Stephanie was distressed, but dry-eyed and philosophical. 'I know I'll be getting some strange looks from people,' she said to Michael.

'They'll all be thinking why a recently married and young man did what he did, and whether his wife had something to do with it.' She avoided the words 'suicide' and 'kill'.

'It was beyond me, Michael, out of my control,' and she reached for him. 'I couldn't go on like that,' and less certainly, 'You do believe that, don't you?'

He held and stroked her. 'Yes, Steph,' he answered. 'No one's going to blame you. For someone to suicide, they'd have to be glutted in heart and mind. People, at least people who matter, will know you're not the reason. They'd know he would have had problems before…before you came along.'

'It's more important, Michael, that you know it, and even more important that I know it.'

Michael was tempted to tell her about Troy's final admission, the killing of his father. It might help her understand the scale of Troy's emotional torment, and release her from any responsibility she felt. But even with Troy gone, he felt that it would be a betrayal.

Troy's mother was less philosophical and blamed herself. It was the first time Michael had been to her new home and met Adrian. She dabbed at her eyes with a wet handkerchief for most of his visit, while Adrian, ever attentive, stood behind her with his hand on her shoulder. Michael had always liked Beth Douglas, and was pleased she'd found a happier life.

'Why, Michael, why?' she pleaded, believing he knew her son better than anyone. 'I know things weren't all that good for him as a child, but he'd found a lovely girl, they hadn't been married long. We were so happy for him, weren't we, Adrian?' and she half-turned and tapped the hand that Adrian had resting on her shoulder.

'It's hard to know what's going on in someone else's mind,' Michael answered, deliberately evasive. 'Sometimes it's the person who seems the happiest and most confident, the one you'd least expect.'

He knew it was a trite answer, but Beth Douglas seemed to accept it.

'You're right, of course,' she said, 'how can we know, but if only I'd stood up to Brett, or done something more to make sure Troy…'

'But there was nothing more you could have done, Beth.' Adrian came to the rescue. 'Nothing at all,' and he massaged both her shoulders.

'We knew he'd left Stephanie, such a nice girl, and we never knew why, what happened between them, but he told us it was only temporary, that they'd had some differences and would be back together soon… What do you young ones call it? Needing your own space. Well, we begged him to come and stay with us. He'd have had his own room, home-cooked meals… Adrian was willing to make him feel at home at the golf club…'

Michael left, promising to keep in touch. Beth hugged him. Adrian took his offered hand in both of his.

He knew it was too easy to be critical of Beth, to say that she should have stood up to her abusing husband. She'd have been asking for more punishment for both of them. And if she had left him, where could she have gone? How could she have lived?

He felt unusually sad, sad because he'd lost his best friend in a tragic way, and sad because of the purgative of time. He knew that life's experiences disappear almost as soon as they happen, hurtling away to a negligent past so that we can scarcely remember the heat of the day, the chirruping of birds, the tang of salt spray on bare arms, or the pain of something tragic.

There'd always be poignant moments for Beth, but she had Adrian, and time would work its magic.

Ealing Clinic was situated on Sydney's North Shore, a three-storey neat building between expensive homes and tall gums, and like those homes, it suggested the province of the well-to-do. It was a couple of blocks away from the heavy traffic of the main road that lead to the more-pricey suburbs. Michael wasn't sure of its mission, but gathered that it provided both medical and psychiatric support.

When he entered with Deirdre, who insisted that he come and

wouldn't take no for an answer, he found an elegant décor in shades of grey leading to spacious corridors, and a courteous receptionist. He imagined a smell of sickness, but knew that his mind was playing tricks. Perhaps it was the smell of love denied.

'Tiffany Thurgood,' Deirdre said brightly, leaning over the receptionist's desk.

'Room thirteen,' the receptionist answered, eyeing Deirdre's encroachment on her desk with disapproval. 'She's expecting you,' and she gave directions.

Turning a corner in the corridor, they nearly ran into a naked man with a vacant look, a shock of white hair, ridiculously skinny legs, and a penis that nestled in a bird's nest of hair like an unchaste rose. Two embarrassed nurses hurried him away.

Room thirteen, like all the others along the corridor, had a polished door, with a small insert bearing Tiffany's name.

She smiled weakly when they entered. Deirdre rushed to the bed and hugged her, half-lifting her in the bed, exposing her thin bony frame, and smoothing her hair. Michael, less demonstrative, waited till Deirdre had retreated, and kissed her lightly on the cheek.

She looked almost white, and the colour and light had gone from her eyes. Her hair was dull. A single sheet seemed to shroud a diminished body, a shell.

'How's it going, Tiff?' Deirdre was jolly. 'Do you think being here is doing you good?'

'I think so.' Her answer was slow in coming and barely audible.

'Wonderful. You're looking better.' Deirdre was altogether too loud and gushy. 'Now, I reckon you want all the gossip. Right?'

Tiffany gave a barely perceptible nod. She was looking at Michael. 'Shut up, Deirdre,' he wanted to say, but didn't.

'Deirdre,' Michael said, 'perhaps if we each have a few minutes alone…'

'Got it!' Deirdre said breezily, winked at Michael, and left the room. 'Behave yourselves now,' she called from the doorway.

Michael sat on the bed, and took Tiffany's hand. They didn't talk for some time. Silence seemed enough.

'I'm sorry, Michael.'

He had to lean over her to hear.

'I wasn't very kind. It wasn't fair, was it?'

'Time's up!' Deirdre returned ablaze and pointed Michael to the door. 'It's the turn of the girls.'

He'd started to really dislike her. He left reluctantly. Tiffany watched him go. He had more to say. He wanted to tell her that it wasn't all bad. There were some good times. It wasn't for him, the callous sequel of love when every memory is recreated as hurt.

He went back along the corridor, passed the receptionist, who gave him an enquiring look, and sat in the car to wait. Deirdre could find him. He wouldn't go back. Not now. Not ever.

He wasn't sure why he decided after a month to revisit Govett's Leap. It was a spur of the moment decision. It wasn't some ghoulish desire to see where it happened. It was more like a sentimental pilgrimage. Like people visiting a relative's grave. A chance to feel close. To honour the dead.

He needed to do it alone, so he told no one, and took nothing except the old travelling rug that lived in the boot. He intended to return that same night.

It was early afternoon, hot and ming blue when he left, wondering what sort of day it was when Troy had gone. Was it a sacred canvas of blue like today? Were clouds bullying the sky? Did it mean anything to Troy, or were his senses long dead to what the natural world had to offer?

The traffic was busy along the M4. Cars sped by at alarming speed, switching lanes with reckless abandon. Truck horns blared. A helicopter droned overhead. He turned on the car radio to mask the noise, and wondered if it was a mistake to come. But when he reached Emu Plains, the traffic thinned, and as he climbed, he smelled a crispness in the mountain air. He could breathe. He could think.

Images formed, made their claim and disappeared. The infant Michael bleeding into his socks while Mummy coddled the less injured Amity, the cool, delicious hands of Narelle and Sylvia in primary school folk dancing, the girl-deprived and imagined mediaeval conquests in his teenage years, the date with leggy Clara that firmed his ideal, and later, the gentle attentions of his near-immaculate relationship with Stephanie.

And somewhere in there, sex came marching in with its implacable demands. But how to fit it in to his scheme of things? Easy. Make it the supreme ideal, the ultimate romance. The twining of love and sex.

He loved Tiffany, but wasn't able to express what he felt, wasn't permitted to express what he felt. The ideal remained, and became even more meaningful with denial and the passage of time, but it was unfulfilled, until one Saturday night the dream was shattered.

And for Tiffany, it wasn't even him in the bed that night. Her love-making was frenzied. It was Paul she was taking, and with a misplaced fury. Her love had to go on living, as strong in death as in life, just as to deny a living love between Grace and Alan was beyond understanding.

Blaxland, lower Blue Mountains, and running beside the railway line, a crowded shopping centre in the main street much like that in any suburb, not yet what he considered the real Blue Mountains.

Troy had told him that Tiffany had become his obsession. He was right. What was it that made a person attracted to another? What long-nursed ideal? What unmet need? What spread of complementary chemicals? Was his epiphany a disenchantment with her, or a growing knowledge of himself? He knew the answer now.

He'd known girls who'd teased his heart, or groin, but not his mind. He'd known girls who'd stirred his mind, and nothing else. Shouldn't a workable relationship be a blend of all those?

Why Tiffany? What magic did she have for him? He couldn't say. You can't reason love. But can you reason obsession? He had…hadn't he?

Faulconbridge, and not nearly as dense now, fewer shops, a crispness in the air, and more of what's distinctive about the old-world charm of the mountains, whatever that is. He stopped for a takeaway to drink on the way.

Stephanie wanted to be reminded of the quote about monsters. Nietzsche went on to say that if you spent too long looking into the abyss, the abyss will look back at you. Wasn't that Troy's obsession? He spent so long looking into the abyss, it finally claimed him. He'd have liked the irony of that, of literally stepping into the abyss.

But what happened to him as a child might not have been his obsession. He might not have had an obsession at all. Who was to know? Even he wasn't sure. With age, the difference between truth and fiction becomes less certain. And the present always wants to patronise the past, pretend it has all the answers.

Blackheath at last, and Michael drove down Govett's Leap Road to the look out and Bridal Veil Falls. He sat in the car for several minutes, listening to the bush sounds, and watching the gum leaves, a gentle agitation in the lethargy of afternoon. He was in no hurry.

It was important to experience the feel of it all. He wondered if Troy had done the same.

Closing the car door, he went to the lookout, leant against the railing, and feeling the roasting afternoon sun on his face, looked across the blue haze of mountains.

'Have you seen Wally?' An infant girl in a party frock with Shirley Temple curls was pushing a stuffed toy that looked like a wombat against his thigh, and was looking up at him with entreating blue eyes. 'Would you like to hold him?'

'Emily,' a woman rushed over, laughing, 'leave that poor man alone.'

'I'd love to hold Wally,' Michael answered.

After a minute of chat with the silent Wally, he thanked the satisfied girl and her mother, and walked the few hundred metres towards the falls.

'Just there,' a man said in passing.

'I beg your pardon.'

'That spot. Sorry, but I thought you might be looking.' He pointed to the fence. 'Where the fellow went over a month back. Did you hear about it?'

'Yes…thank you.'

Michael waited until the man had gone, his wish to rehash the story thwarted. No one else was around, and he climbed the fence, standing well away from the edge. It was the end of the world, a sea of blue, sky and mountains. No one came. It was late afternoon. He found the cool mountain air bracing. The falls were roaring. It had rained the night before.

It was all so familiar. The sky across the valley slowly turning mauve and charcoal, the sun making its final protest by dousing him in slants of light before it retired for another day.

He wasn't sure how long he stood there. Time had lost its meaning, but he gradually became aware of someone standing by his side, a definite presence. It was no mirage, no trick of his imagination. He didn't look. He felt like he was waking from a dream. They stood together, without speaking, close but not touching, looking at the sun giving a final pink capitulating breath.

'I hear the Gardners Inn does a great roast of the day,' Stephanie said.